SANTA CRUZ BANDIDOS

The gruesome sight of a young man hanging from a tree in the Mexican village of Santa Cruz arouses Brogan McNally's emotions and curiosity. He discovers that a local bandido named Pablo Santos has threatened to hang all the young men in the village unless a cache of money, alleged to have been hidden there, is handed over. True to his nature, Brogan leads the villagers against Santos. He is also forced to help the Mexican army search for him. But when the army detachment is ambushed by Santos, Brogan must continue alone . . .

Books by L. D. Tetlow
in the Linford Western Library:

BROGAN: TO EARN A DOLLAR
THIRTEEN DAYS
BROGAN AND THE JUDGE KILLER
GRINGO
MAVERICK
PITIQUITO TRAIL
GRIZZLY
THE BOUNTY TRAIL
SQUAW HUNTERS

L. D. TETLOW

SANTA CRUZ BANDIDOS

Complete and Unabridged

LINFORD
Leicester

First published in Great Britain in 2003 by
Robert Hale Limited
London

First Linford Edition
published 2005
by arrangement with
Robert Hale Limited
London

British Library CIP Data

Tetlow, L. D.
    Santa Cruz bandidos.—Large print ed.—
Linford western library
    1. McNally, Brogan (Fictitous character)—
Fiction 2. Western stories 3. Large type books
    I. Title
    823.9′14 [F]

    ISBN 1–84395–767–1

Published by
F. A. Thorpe (Publishing)
Anstey, Leicestershire
Set by Words & Graphics Ltd.
Anstey, Leicestershire
Printed and bound in Great Britain by
T. J. International Ltd., Padstow, Cornwall

This book is printed on acid-free paper

1

The small Mexican village appeared completely deserted. Deserted that was except for two small, yapping dogs and a body hanging from a tree in the centre of the square outside the church. The body swung slightly in the wind, its eyes bulging but unseeing. There was no need for Brogan to examine the body to confirm that the man was dead.

It was also plain that the hanging had taken place not all that long before Brogan had arrived on the scene. Immediately his hand slipped to the Colt in his holster as he looked about for signs of life but, apart from the two dogs, the village remained stubbornly silent.

He also knew very well that at that precise moment unseen faces were staring at him. What he did not know was whether or not those responsible for the young man's death — he was obviously a very young man, probably in his late teens — were still around and amongst the eyes trained upon him. Cautiously he rode the few yards to a hitching rail outside a white-painted building bearing the name 'Cantina'.

Gun now at the ready, he dismounted, hitched his horse to the rail and after pausing for a few moments as he looked about, slowly pushed open the door of the cantina. He remained outside, flattened against the wall, fully expecting a volley of shots but none came.

'Anybody in there?' he called out.

There was no reply but the faintest of sounds from inside told him that there was somebody inside. Once again, very cautiously, he peered through the now open doorway. Another slight sound and he suddenly stepped inside.

'Please, *señor*,' came a croaking voice, 'Do not shoot.'

'Show yourself!' commanded Brogan. 'You have nothing to fear from me.'

Very slowly four shadowy figures emerged from behind an upturned table, their hands raised. They moved forward into the light and proved to be three old men and an elderly woman.

'What the hell's goin' on here?' demanded Brogan.

'You are *Americano*?' croaked one of the men.

'Well I sure ain't no Mexican,' replied Brogan. 'I repeat my question. What the hell's goin' on here?'

'You are not with Pablo Santos?' said the man.

'Never heard of him,' said Brogan. 'My name's McNally, Brogan McNally an' I ain't with nobody.'

'Then you would be most wise to continue your journey, Señor McNally,' said the old man. 'Santa Cruz is not a healthy place for anyone at this moment.'

'I can see that by the body of the young man outside,' said Brogan. 'Now would you mind tellin' me what's goin' on?' He holstered his Colt in an effort

3

to reassure the old man.

'That is the work of Pablo Santos and his men,' said the old man. 'Jose was the second of our young men to be hanged. The first one was two days ago.'

'And why should this Pablo Santos want to hang 'em?' asked Brogan.

'I think perhaps it might be safer for you if you did not concern yourself with our problems,' said the old man.

'You're probably quite right about that,' agreed Brogan. 'My trouble is I can't help myself from pokin' my nose in things. I see you have a church, is your priest about? Maybe he'll tell me what's goin' on.'

'Sí, Padre Luis Salada,' said the old man. 'He too has been badly injured by Santos, but he is not dead. He is in the house behind the church. Santos beat him three days ago. It was feared that he would die.'

'Take me to him,' ordered Brogan. 'I don't want one of your people gettin' the wrong idea an' tryin' to kill me. Where is this Pablo Santos now?'

'*Sí*, Señor McNally,' agreed the old man. 'I will take you to him. Santos, he is not far away. He and his men are in the hills behind the village. He does not stay in the village because he does not want to risk the army finding him. They come into our village regularly.'

'And from what I've seen of the Mexican army I don't suppose you want them here either,' said Brogan. 'I take it this Santos is an outlaw and the army are after him?'

'*Sí*, he is what you Americano's call an outlaw, what we call a *bandido*,' said the old man. 'He broke out of prison and has been on the run for about two months now. The army are looking for him but I think they do not look too hard. When we told them where he was they rode off in the opposite direction. They do not appear concerned about what Santos might do to us.'

'That figures,' said Brogan. 'OK, take me to your priest.'

'If that is what you wish, *señor*,' agreed the old man.

5

'I suppose I ought to just ride on like you said,' said Brogan. 'Still, now I'm here I might as well know what's goin' on.'

Brogan was led across the square and past the church to a house which was slightly larger than most of the others. As they crossed the square Brogan was aware of faces peering through dingy windows and round half-open doors. At the house they were met by a youngish woman who looked at Brogan with a mixture of terror and curiosity. The old man spoke to her in Spanish. She nodded briefly and led them inside, through the small first room and into an even smaller bedroom.

A bandaged figure, whom Brogan took to be Padre Luis Salada, peered at his visitors for a moment, reached for a pair of spectacles and after putting them on and adjusting them slightly, once again peered at Brogan. The old man spoke to him, again in Spanish.

'So you are Señor McNally,' said the priest. 'Please forgive me for not greeting you properly but as you can see I am not really fit to greet anyone. What can I do for you, Señor McNally?'

'You can tell me just why that young man is hanging from that tree out there,' said Brogan.

The priest glanced at the woman standing at his bedside for a brief instant. 'Jose?' he queried. She looked at him briefly, lowered her eyes and nodded. 'I thought so,' he continued. 'First Manuel and now Jose. I was not told they had hanged Jose. Manuel and Jose are . . . were brothers, the grand-sons of the village headman. Pablo Santos told us that he would hang one young man each day until he had the information or the money he wanted. He could not do so yesterday since the army were here.'

'What information and what money?' asked Brogan.

'Perhaps I should ask you what your interest in this matter is?' said the priest. 'We do not know you, señor. We

7

do not know if you have been sent by Santos or not. Please explain yourself.'

'Seems to me it ain't me who need explain a thing,' said Brogan. 'All I know is I just happened to come across this village and find a young man hangin' from a tree. Call me nosy if you like, but I'm just curious. It ain't every day I come across folk hangin' from trees. Still, I guess I know when I'm not wanted so I'll just be on my way.'

'It would perhaps be the wisest thing you could do,' said the priest. 'I hear that Pablo Santos does not care very much for gringos, especially *Americanos*.'

'OK,' shrugged Brogan. 'If nobody wants to tell me I guess I can't force 'em. Personally I don't care if this Santos burns down your whole village, rapes all your women an' girls an' hangs all your men.'

The priest studied Brogan for a few moments and then smiled.

'I do not think so, Señor McNally,' he said. 'I believe that you do care. It shows in your voice and in your face. Why you should, I do not know, you place yourself in great danger.'

'Danger seems to have been the story of my life so far,' said Brogan. 'I've lost count of the number of times men have tried to kill me, just as I've lost count of the number of men who ended up dead tryin'.'

'*Sí*, you have the manner and appearance of a man who knows how to handle a gun and is not afraid to use it, but you do not look like a killer,' said the priest. 'I do not mean that you will not kill or have not killed a man or many men, but you do not seem like a man who kills for a living or without good cause.'

'I like to think not,' said Brogan. 'OK, Padre, so satisfy my curiosity and tell me just why this Pablo Santos is hangin' your young men.'

'Money, Señor McNally,' said the priest with a wry smile. 'Much money, all in American dollars, or so he would claim.' He looked at the woman and the old man and nodded. 'Please leave us, I will talk with Señor McNally alone. Do not concern yourselves, I believe I will be safe with Señor McNally.'

The old man and the woman left the room and the house and for a few minutes Padre Salada remained silent.

'I'm waitin', Padre,' said Brogan.

'First, I must ask you just why you wish to know?' said the priest. 'As I say, we do not know if you have been sent by Santos or not. We are talking about American dollars, so what would be more logical than to send an American, perhaps claiming to be from the American government, to try and recover the money?'

'The nearest I ever got to the American government was when I once took on the job of sheriff for a while,' said Brogan. 'That didn't work out. I'm what we call a saddle tramp, padre, a drifter. I don't owe nothin' to nobody, I don't work for nobody 'ceptin' myself an' you can believe me or not, as you choose, I ain't never stole nothin' off nobody an' I ain't never murdered nobody. Sure, I've killed my share of men but they all deserved it or it was in self-defence.'

'And I choose to believe you, Señor McNally,' said the priest. 'Very well, I will tell you what happened . . . '

Padre Salada explained that Pablo Santos had escaped from prison a few months earlier and had suddenly turned up in the village of Santa Cruz demanding to know where $100,000 in American money was hidden. Apparently whilst in prison he had been told that the money, the proceeds of a robbery across the border, was hidden in Santa Cruz.

'In truth I do not know anything about this money,' said the priest. 'Santos refused to believe me or any of the people here. He even forced the villagers to dig in all likely places but we found nothing. He still refused to believe that we know nothing and three days ago he told us that unless we produced the money or told him where

11

it was, he would hang one young man each day until we did tell him. He said that when all the young men and boys had been hanged he would start hanging all the young women and girls but that it would be worse for them since he would turn his men loose on each of them before they were hanged.'

'There must be more than one village called Santa Cruz,' said Brogan. 'It's a common enough name. If you know nothing, he obviously got the wrong place.'

'This we pointed out to him,' said the priest. 'However he insisted that this was the right village and that we must know about it. He claims that the man he met in prison was quite specific about the village but that he did not know exactly where the money was hidden.'

'How long have you been here, Padre?' asked Brogan. 'Maybe it was before your time.'

'Ten years next month,' said the

priest. 'I do not think it happened more than ten years ago. In fact Santos says that the money was stolen from across the border only three years ago.'

'Well if he is right then surely something must have happened in the village since then,' said Brogan. 'You must have had strangers through in that time. Can't you think of anything that might have happened in that time, especially about three years ago?'

'I have given the matter much thought,' said the priest. 'The villagers too have given the matter much thought but they can come up with nothing. It is true that about that time we did have three men, *Americanos*, come to the village for a few days, but they were no trouble and we did not see them hiding anything.'

'And you've searched everywhere?' urged Brogan.

'*Sí*, we have searched all the likely places and many not so likely,' said the priest. 'We found nothing but Santos refuses to believe us.'

'Have you told the army?' asked Brogan.

'*Sí*, we have told them but they do not seem interested.' sighed the priest. 'There you have the full story, Señor McNally. Our problem is how to convince Santos that we know nothing.'

'OK, so you can't convince him,' said Brogan. 'Why don't your men band together and use guns against Santos?'

The priest gave a wry smile and straightened himself in the bed before replying.

'The people of this village are but poor farmers,' he said. 'They cannot afford guns and they are not gunfighters. It would also seem that Santos anticipated such a thing. His men searched every house and every building, including the church and took away every gun in the village which was not many. A few old shotguns only.'

'That figures,' said Brogan. 'So what do you intend doing about this Santos? You can't just let him hang all your young men.'

'Without any means of protecting ourselves, what can we do?' said the priest with a deep sigh. 'We can only put our trust in God.'

'I don't think God is goin' to be much help,' said Brogan. 'Not unless he can show you where the money is or send down some guns.'

'Do not mock the way of the Lord,' said the priest. 'You are plainly not a religious man, Señor McNally.'

'That don't make me a bad man though,' said Brogan. 'At least I don't think so. I've been driftin' long enough to have more faith in my own intuition and my guns than in any god.'

'True, it does not mean that you are a bad man, Señor McNally,' agreed the priest. 'But every man needs something in which to believe. If he has no faith or beliefs then what has he to live for?'

'That kind of talk is too deep for me, Padre,' said Brogan. 'So, you put your trust in your god, do nothing and hope. In the meantime Santos continues to murder all your people. I would have thought that there are times when even your god needs some sort of help.'

'Perhaps you can suggest a way?' said the priest. 'I have tried to find other ways but we cannot argue against Santos and his guns.'

'So which is more powerful, a bullet or your faith?' asked Brogan. 'Don't get me wrong, Padre, I respect your beliefs and your faith but even they have to be backed up by force sometimes.'

'This we know,' said the priest. 'But as you say, our faith alone will not protect us from the bullet, Señor McNally. I appreciate your concern but truly, what can you do about it? You will soon be on your way, that is your nature. You will then leave us as we were before you arrived, at the mercy of Pablo Santos. I do not expect you to help us, we are not your concern but I thank you.'

'Well I'll be around for a couple of days yet,' said Brogan. 'My horse needs a rest and so do I.'

'Then I pray, for your sake, that

Santos stays away,' said the priest. 'You are most welcome to what little we have and I am sure we can find somewhere for both you and your horse to rest. I suspect that you are a man who is well used to sleeping under the stars but I think we can do something better than that. Tell the old man who brought you here that he is to find you accommodation. By the way, the two young men who have so far died, they were his grandsons.'

'Many thanks,' said Brogan. 'But I don't mind sleepin' out in the open, I've been doin' that for most of my life. I would appreciate some decent food though. I haven't had a good meal for more'n two weeks.'

'They will provide food at the cantina,' said the priest. 'Do not, however, expect anything too rich or lavish. We are simple people and live and eat in a simple manner. I hope you like maize or rice.'

'Sounds better'n rattlesnake or lizard tails to me,' said Brogan.

The old man was waiting outside and he escorted Brogan back to the cantina where a drink of indeterminate origin was placed in front of him. However, although slightly sweet, it tasted quite good. The old man said that he would see to it that his horse was fed and watered and dispatched a young boy to lead it away.

Eventually a large platter of rice, maize and what proved to be mainly vegetables with a little meat which he suspected was goat, all well seasoned with spices, was placed in front of him. Although rather too spicy for his taste, Brogan knew that to refuse it would be an insult to his hosts and ate it all as though he was really enjoying it. At first the old man refused to accept payment but Brogan insisted by forcing a dollar piece into his hand. The money was immediately taken away and Brogan knew that it would be well hidden.

'What about this money that was supposed to have been hidden here?' Brogan eventually asked the old man.

'Can't you think of anything?'

'*Señor*,' replied the old man. 'I have given the matter much thought and I can think of nothing. It is true that shortly after the money was supposed to have been stolen, three men arrived here and stayed a few days, but as far as we know they did not hide anything.'

'The three men,' said Brogan. 'What happened to them?'

'They left the village and that was the last we saw or heard of them,' said the old man. 'Perhaps it was one of these men whom Santos claims to have met in prison, but I do not know. They seemed to be good men, they were no trouble at all and did not try to force themselves upon our women. One of them was obviously a religious man since he spent much time praying in the church. The other two did not appear to be interested.'

Brogan thought about that last remark. It could have been as the old man had said, that one of the men was religious, but somehow it did not ring true. He did not voice his opinion but he resolved to look in the church. He had no doubt that it had been thoroughly searched but there might have been something they had missed.

Before he could do anything, however, a small boy came in and spoke to the old man in Spanish. The old man nodded sadly at the woman and then at Brogan. 'You will have to excuse us, Señor McNally,' he said. 'We are about to bury my grandson. He is the one you found hanging from the tree.'

Brogan did not say anything but he did follow them out of the cantina. Quite suddenly, it seemed, the village had come to life. He estimated that there were at least two hundred people of all ages now gathered in the square. He tried to remember if the body had been cut down before he went into the cantina but, unusually for him, he had not noticed.

Padre Luis Salada had managed to get out of his bed and was now dressed in his white robes and waiting at the church door. Outside the church, on the ground, was a rough coffin. Slowly the whole crowd moved towards the church and the coffin was picked up and carried inside, followed by the crowd. Brogan chose to remain outside, not wishing to intrude on their grief.

He could hear the sounds of the service as he walked around the church, looking at various parts of it with renewed interest. It was not an interest in the architecture but an interest in looking for likely hiding places. At the same time he was questioning his own role in the matter.

The most obvious answer was for him to move on. Much as he might sympathize with the villagers, the purely practical part of him acknowledged that there was little he could do. It seemed obvious to him that the villagers simply did not know anything about the money and it was equally possible that there was no money. Santa Cruz was not an uncommon name and it was quite possible that Pablo Santos was quite wrong. Being wrong however, was of no help at all to the villagers.

He considered his position and decided that he would do as planned and remain for another two days and then be on his way. If Pablo Santos should happen to arrive in that time, he decided that he might attempt to reason with him. However, he had come across Mexican *bandidos* before and had always found them to be rather single-minded and unreasonable. He was not too worried about not being able to deal with Santos should the need arise.

By the time he had walked completely round the church, the service had ended and everyone was gathered in the small graveyard. He stood and watched as the coffin was lowered into the ground. He did notice that it was only at that point that the elderly woman from the cantina, plainly the grandmother of the youth, started to cry, as did two much younger women whom he took to be close relatives.

Gradually the crowd dispersed and Brogan entered the church.

It was much like thousands of other village churches in Mexico. As with other communities, the church was spotlessly clean and apparently recently whitewashed. The altar was plainer than some and it appeared obvious that none of the objects on or around the altar were of any great value. For a few moments he stood and tried to imagine what the man who might have arrived with the money would have looked at and what he had been thinking. His thoughts were suddenly interrupted by a slight sound behind him.

'I do not think you contemplate the Lord,' said Padre Luis Salada.

'No, I don't,' admitted Brogan. 'Padre, you didn't tell me that one of the men who arrived all that time ago spent a great deal of his time in here.'

'The doors are always open,' said the priest. 'Even men like that are not above belief in the Lord.'

'Even men like what?' asked Brogan.

'He was obviously a man who was used to killing,' said the priest. 'Believe me, I have what you call a nose for these things. You too have that same aura but with him it was different. I believe he killed people for pleasure. Oh, it is quite true that he did nothing whilst he was here, but I sense these things.'

'And did you sense that he believed in God?' asked Brogan.

'I sensed that his only god was money,' said the priest. 'Oh, I know what it is you are thinking, Señor McNally. When I heard about the theft of the money I too had the same thought and I searched every part of this church but found nothing. I now believe that the three men we saw were the men who stole the money but I do not believe that they chose this church or this village to hide it. I am quite certain that we would have found it by now had that been the case.'

'Maybe so,' said Brogan. 'Tell me, Padre, what would you have done with the money if you had found it? Indeed, what would you do with it if you found it now? It's a lot of money and I have no doubt that your village could put it to good use.'

'The devil puts many temptations in our way,' said the priest with a wry smile. 'Who is to know what one would really do until faced with the choice. The first time you had to kill a man, señor, what did you feel before you squeezed that trigger?'

'Bloody sore!' laughed Brogan. 'He'd almost beaten me to a pulp and was about to finish me off with a shot to the head. I don't even remember shooting him, but they told me that's what happened. I acted out of instinct.'

'Then all I can say is that I must let instinct and God dictate what action I would take,' replied the priest with another wry smile.

'Are you sure you haven't done that already?' asked Brogan.

'I understand you, Señor McNally,' said the priest. 'But no, as yet I have not had to rely on instinct.'

2

'And now I must rest,' said the priest. 'My body is no longer that of a young man and cannot quickly recover from the beating which Santos inflicted upon it. I will leave you to your meditations, Señor McNally. Perhaps you will take the opportunity to reflect on the ways of the Lord, but I do not think so. I suspect that you look for possible hiding-places for the money. I wish you luck but I do not think you will discover any hiding-place. Believe me, these past few days we have searched everywhere.'

'Maybe a fresh pair of eyes might see something you've missed,' said Brogan. 'I also have the advantage that I don't have the limited outlook of the likes of the people in this village. I can think with the mind of an outlaw.'

'*Think* with the mind of an outlaw, *sí*,' agreed the priest, 'but I do not believe that you *act* with the mind of an outlaw. If I can be of any assistance, you know where to find me. My door is always open.'

'Just one thought,' said Brogan. 'You said that the two young men were the *grandsons* of the village headman. What happened to their parents? I didn't see anybody at the funeral who looked like his mother or father.'

'Sadly, they both died of the fever four years ago,' sighed the priest. 'There was a bad fever throughout the village and more than twenty people died. That kind of thing we accept, it is the will of God, but what is happening now is different.'

'Different?' queried Brogan. 'Surely you must believe that whatever happens is the will of God? I know I don't but that's how a lot of folk think.'

'Perhaps so,' said the priest. 'But even if such a belief is accepted, it does not make it any the easier to bear. I have been a priest for many years, Señor McNally, and even I find it difficult to

27

accept such things at times. Now, I must leave you. A room has been prepared for you at the cantina. It is not much but it is all we can offer. Also, a word of advice. Should Pablo Santos or any of his men come into the village while you are here, I would suggest that you keep to your room and do not interfere with anything they do.'

'Even if they try to hang another of your young men?' asked Brogan.

'I think only of your interests, *señor*,' said the priest. 'They would most certainly kill you and your death would be totally unnecessary.'

'I agree, it would be totally unnecessary,' said Brogan. 'I'll think about it, but I don't know if I can just stand by and watch.'

'You are a good man, *señor*,' sighed the priest. 'I simply point out that any intervention might result in your death.'

Padre Luis Salada left the church and Brogan considered the advice he had been given. However, much as he wanted to avoid trouble and most certainly the possibility of his being killed, he did not feel that he could simply stand by whilst another young man was hanged.

Turning his attention back to the interior of the church and a possible hiding-place, he wandered around prodding at walls and examining the few statues which were there. The altar quite plainly offered no possibilities since it consisted of nothing more than a flat, sandstone slab set into the back wall and supported by two narrow sandstone legs. He did tap at all three pieces of sandstone, hoping to find that one of them was hollow, but they were quite plainly very solid. In the end he was forced to agree that there was nowhere inside the church which could have been used as a hiding-place. That meant that if the money was there somewhere, it must be outside.

Once again he walked all round the church and although he discovered one or two loose blocks, they proved to be just that, loose blocks. At the door his eyes travelled up to the bell which was housed above it and consisted of nothing more than a narrow stone structure. However, he did find a ladder of sorts and climbed up to examine the bell and its housing. Once again, there was nowhere where anybody could have hidden anything.

Most of that afternoon was spent with him wandering about the village examining buildings and even looking under rocks, all to no avail. Eventually he decided that Pablo Santos must have been given the wrong information. As far as he was concerned there was no money hidden anywhere.

On returning to the cantina, he was shown his room — little more than a cubby-hole but large enough — and another helping of the same spicy food he had eaten earlier was placed in front of him. Once again he ate it as though he were enjoying it and had to admit that it really did not taste too bad. The night passed uneventfully and Brogan slept well.

★ ★ ★

The night might have passed without incident but almost as the first rays of dawn broke, there was obvious panic in the village.

'Santos!' gasped the old man. 'He comes, you must hide.'

'Hide?' said Brogan, straightening himself to his full height. 'Brogan McNally ain't never run scared from nobody in his life an' he ain't about to start now.'

'But Santos, he hates all gringos,' said the old man. 'He will kill you.'

'He can try,' said Brogan.

He had to admit to himself that he was acting out of little more than pure pig-headedness and realized that there was some sense in not making his presence obvious — at least not for the moment. He returned to his small room and peered through a tiny window which overlooked the square.

A few minutes later seven men on horseback galloped into the village which was, by that time, completely deserted. A surprisingly small man leapt off his horse and stood in the centre of the square for a few minutes, looking round. He gave a nod to his men who then also dismounted and started to go from house to house, herding the villagers out into the square. One of them even came into the cantina and forced the old man and woman out but he did not look in the room occupied by Brogan.

Eventually all the villagers, including Padre Luis Salada, were assembled and Santos addressed them in Spanish. Brogan's knowledge of Spanish was very limited so he obviously could not understand what was being said, although he had a fairly good idea just what the subject was.

When he had finished addressing the villagers, Santos said something to one of his men and suddenly a youth was snatched from the crowd. A woman, obviously his mother, screamed out and fell to her knees as she pleaded with

Santos. A man Brogan took to be the father of the youth tried his best to comfort her.

As the youth was led — strangely submissive and quiet — towards the tree, Padre Salada also started to plead with Santos. This appeared to cause the *bandido* some amusement at first but he suddenly lost patience and kicked the priest to the ground. He pointed his gun at the padre's head and shouted something at the crowd. They went very quiet. Eventually he laughed and slipped his gun back into his belt and followed the youth to the tree.

The rope used for the previous day's hanging was still there, although now on the ground and the *bandido* who had led the youth to the tree threw it over a branch and dragged the youth closer where he slipped the noose over his head. Santos once again spoke to the villagers but apart from the wailings and pleadings of the boy's mother, all remained sullenly silent. Santos laughed loudly and said something to his men.

Two of them joined the first man and took hold of the rope . . .

★ ★ ★

Brogan's shot was not intended to kill anyone but it was intended to injure. One of the men about to haul on the rope screamed out in pain and snatched his hand away. The other two let the rope drop along with the youth and all seven men were snatching at their guns and looking about in panic.

'That's about as far as you go this time, Santos,' Brogan called through the now broken window to his room. 'I could just as easy kill you or any of your men but I don't want to, leastways not for the moment.'

Santos said something to one of the villagers but did not move. '*Americano*, eh!' he called to Brogan. 'I do not like *Americano* gringos. This is none of your business, gringo. You would be well advised not to interfere. That way perhaps you might live a little longer.'

'I guess I just made it my business,' called Brogan. 'I know what you want but I think you got it all wrong. There ain't no money here. You got the wrong Santa Cruz.'

'I see,' laughed Santos. 'You too have come for the money and want it all for yourself. I know it is here, gringo and I intend to get it. Even if I have to kill everyone in this filthy village, I will find the money. Pablo Santos always gets what he wants. I do not have the wrong village, gringo. I got the information from one of the men who originally stole the money when I too was in prison. It seems he killed his *campadres* so that he could take it all himself. Unfortunately he died before he could tell me exactly where it was. I do not like gringos but perhaps that was one time when I should not have beaten him so hard. It is here, I know it and I will find it even if I have to pull every building down.'

'Not if you're dead you won't,' called Brogan. 'I can pick you all off quite easily. In fact I probably ought to do just that. It'd sure save these poor folk a whole heap of bother. Hangin' these folk ain't goin' to help none. They don't know where it is, but I guess you is too bone-headed to realize that. If you're so certain it's here, the only way to find it is dig everythin' up.'

'Your arrival tells me such a thing will be a waste of time,' called Santos. 'By that time you will have found it and taken it away.'

'I don't know any more than you do where it is or even if it's here,' said Brogan. 'Anyhow, that's enough jawin' for now. On your horses an' get the hell out of here. If I was you I wouldn't come back either. I'll be here for a while yet an' I promise you I'll kill anyone who comes anywhere near these folk. Now, on your horses before I change my mind about killing you right now. You can be quite certain that you will be the first, Santos.'

Santos ordered his men to mount up and when they were all astride their horses he called to Brogan.

'This time, gringo,' he said, 'you have the advantage. I can wait for the money but can you afford to wait? I think not. A few more days or even weeks will not matter to me but it will to you. In the meantime remember that Mexico is a big country but it can never be big enough for you to hide. I know this country, gringo. I will find you and when I do your death will be very slow and very painful. I have Apache blood in my veins and I know many ways of ensuring a slow and painful death.'

Brogan's reply was to shoot at Santos. He did not kill him but he knew that he had inflicted a severe graze to the man's cheek. Santos howled with pain, covered the side of his face and galloped out of the village followed by his men.

Brogan ran out of the cantina and, although he had not expected to be mobbed with gratitude, he was surprised at the way the villagers reacted. They now appeared frightened of him.

The only person who showed any gratitude at all was the mother of the youth and even she was held back by her husband.

Brogan stooped over the body of Padre Luis Salada and examined him. He did not appear to be injured any more than he already had been. He was joined by the woman who obviously acted as the padre's housekeeper. Even she now appeared to be very uncertain of Brogan.

'That was most unwise, Señor McNally,' croaked the priest. 'Not only have you now ensured your own death, you have ensured that Santos will now take out further revenge upon us. From this time on I fear for the women of this village. So far he has not molested them but now he well might.'

'Maybe it would have been easier if I had killed him,' said Brogan.

'Easier, sí,' croaked the priest, 'but I could never condone such a thing.'

'I see,' sneered Brogan, turning to the villagers. 'You would all rather have seen this boy hanged. OK, I know when I'm beaten. Why the hell should I bother about any of you or what happens to this village?'

'You are quite wrong, Señor McNally,' said the old man. 'Of course we do not want to see any of our children or anyone else killed. But you must understand that what you have just done can only make things worse for us. Now Santos will not stop at killing our young men one at a time, he is likely to return and rape our women and then slaughter us all.'

'At least it'll get it over an' done with,' said Brogan. 'OK, like I said, I know when I'm beaten. I was goin' to stay a few days but I reckon the best thing I can do now is be on my way. I just don't understand you at all.'

Suddenly the mother of the youth Brogan had just saved struggled free of her husband and ran towards Brogan. She turned and glared at the crowd and then spoke to them in Spanish. The old man translated for Brogan.

'She says it would be better for us all to kill our children and then ourselves,' he said. 'She says that you are right, Señor McNally, and that the time has come to make a stand against Pablo Santos.'

'Does she understand English?' asked Brogan.

'*Sí*, she speaks English,' said the old man, 'but most of our people do not, which is why she speaks to them in Spanish. She now says that it would be better to die fighting Santos than to simply allow him to slaughter us. By resisting him at least we will have died an honourable death.'

'At least she seems to have some guts,' said Brogan. 'What do the others think of that idea?'

'I think they have been shamed,' replied the old man. 'They are shamed by their own thoughts and actions.'

'And you, Padre,' said Brogan, helping Padre Luis Salada to his feet, 'what do you think?'

'I think that perhaps both you and

she are right,' said the priest. 'I did not tell you this before, *señor*, but many of the villagers were talking about leaving the village. They talked of hiding in the hills.'

'And just what good do they think that will do?' asked Brogan. 'You said yourself that these people are only farmers. They wouldn't last a week out there. They would also be easy pickings for Santos, he knows these hills better than they do. No, Padre, the best chance any of them have is to stay here and fight.'

'Fight with what?' asked the priest. 'We do not have any guns. What use are pitchforks against bullets?'

'There are ways,' said Brogan.

'Then perhaps you can teach us these ways,' said the priest. 'She is right about one thing though. It is far better to die trying than to simply stand by and be slaughtered.'

'That's more like it,' said Brogan. 'I was beginning to wonder if any of you had any fire in your bellies.'

'*Sí*,' agreed the priest, 'but it would appear that some of us do have some fire in our bellies. I will speak with them, but it must be left for each to make their own decisions and I must respect those decisions, whatever they might be.'

'Fair enough,' said Brogan. 'But point out to them that taking to the hills is no answer. They will still be completely at the mercy of Santos.'

'*Sí*, Señor McNally,' said the priest. 'I will tell them. Can I also tell them that you will stay and help us?'

'I guess so,' said Brogan. 'If I had any sense at all I'd be on my way out of here right now. I never did have much sense though. My ma always said I was more stubborn than any mule. I guess she was right about that even if she wasn't right about much else.'

'You have no father?' asked the priest.

'Sure, everybody's got a father,' said Brogan. 'I never knew who mine was, that's all. I don't think my ma knew either. She made her money entertainin' sailors up in Seattle.'

Padre Luis Salada smiled and nodded and called to the people. Brogan decided to wander off and look around the church once again. To his surprise he was joined by the mother of the boy.

'You look for the money?' she asked. 'We have all looked for it but have been unable to find it. I only wish that we could find it. That way we could give Pablo Santos what he wants and continue our lives in peace.'

'I look for a possible place for it,' agreed Brogan. 'I've looked once and there doesn't appear to be anywhere it could be. But, I suppose we have to assume that Santos is right and that it is here somewhere.'

'I fear that as far as you are concerned, Señor McNally,' she said, 'even if it is found it will do you no good. You have made an enemy of Pablo Santos and I think that he will now stop at nothing to kill you.'

'He can try,' said Brogan, rather arrogantly. 'Folk have been tryin' to kill me for more years than I care to count, but I'm still here.'

'One day your luck will desert you,' she said.

'Sure, I know that,' said Brogan. 'A bullet in the back or a lucky shot or maybe even comin' across somebody faster'n me. That don't bother me too much, we all got to die sometime.'

'You have no fear of death?'

'No, not of death,' said Brogan. 'Ain't nothin' any of us can do about dyin', it's got to happen to us all sometime. I'd just like it to be quick, that's all. Either that or of old age.'

'I hope it is of old age but it seems most unlikely,' she said. 'I must thank you for what you did for my son. Padre Salada said that it is none of your concern and he is right. I do not understand why you should act the way you do, Señor McNally, but once again I thank you. Your actions have made everybody in the village ashamed, ashamed that a stranger cares more than they seem to.'

'Don't be too hard on them,' said Brogan. 'They are not fighting men, they are farmers and they don't have any guns.'

'People like us might have no guns and we might not be fighters,' she said. 'We are simple folk with simple ways and beliefs but we do have pride if nothing else. That pride does not make their shame any the easier to bear, in fact it makes it harder. We have prayed for guidance these past few days. Perhaps you are the answer to our prayers. No, do not mock, señor. Who knows the ways of God?'

'I ain't mockin',' said Brogan. 'I just don't see me as the answer to nobody's prayers, that's all.'

'We shall see.' She smiled. 'We shall see. Now I shall return and talk to my people. I know there are still a few who would flee to the hills. If that is what they decide I cannot stop them but I agree with you that it would be better to stay and resist Santos.'

Brogan followed her out of the church where he was greeted by Padre Luis Salada. The villagers had begun to disperse and all, including small children, seemed strangely silent. A few smiled weakly and nodded at Brogan as they returned to their homes.

'What did they say, Padre?' asked Brogan.

'They agree to stay and fight,' said the priest. 'They fear the worst and so do I but they know there is little else that they can do. I have called a mass for this evening to pray for success. Perhaps you will join us, Señor McNally?'

'I don't think so, Padre,' said Brogan. 'Somebody up there might get the wrong idea and I wouldn't want that. Are you sure there are no guns anywhere?'

'My father-in-law, Old Carlos, he has an ancient rifle which you call a muzzle-loader,' said the woman. 'However, he does not have any powder or ammunition for it. The last time it was used was more than twenty years ago.'

'I think we can safely rule that out,' said Brogan. 'I'll have to start thinkin'. So far I ain't got the faintest idea what to do, but I'll come up with somethin' even if it's only me ridin' like hell out of here.'

'I do not think you will desert us, Señor McNally,' said the priest with a knowing smile.

'Don't be too sure about that,' said Brogan. 'My own life is far more important to me than *all* the people in this village.'

'Then why is it that you have already risked so much?' the priest asked with another knowing smile.

'A good question, Padre, an' it sure beats me,' said Brogan. 'Still, I reckon you won't be seein' Santos for a while. He knows now that he can't have things all his own way. How long the stand-off will last though, I just don't know. He was right about one thing, he can probably afford to wait longer'n I can.'

'And how long can you afford to wait, Señor McNally?' asked the priest. 'You are of course most welcome to stay amongst us as long as you like.'

'I hope to get somethin' sorted before too long,' said Brogan. 'I guess I'll just have to play things by ear. I'll do me some thinkin' an' I'll talk to the villagers after the mass tonight. I should have somethin' worked out by then — I hope.'

'We are in your hands,' said the priest. 'May God guide you.'

'I don't suppose he will,' said Brogan. 'We ain't been on speakin' terms for a good many years.'

Brogan wandered away from the village studying the layout of the land immediately around it. There seemed to be numerous places where men could be hidden and had they had guns it would have been a fairly simple matter to defend the village — but there were no guns. He sat on the top of a small hill over-looking the village for some time, weighing up all the possibilities.

After a while his attention was drawn to the direction from which Santos had arrived and he noted that he had to pass through a narrow gully about 300 yards away. He went off to examine the approaches.

He climbed to the top of the gully and found that it was slightly less than a quarter of a mile long and at its deepest something over fifty feet. It appeared possible to avoid the direct route through the gully but that apparently involved quite a steep climb and an equally steep drop. He dismissed this as a possible way of attack and decided that a man like Santos would take the direct route — through the gully.

As well as being about fifty feet deep, the gully was also about fifty or sixty feet wide, although it was wider at the approach and slightly narrower at the end. He decided that if they were going to tackle Santos, the only place they would stand any sort of chance of success was when Santos was in the gully.

In the absence of guns, the only weapons at the disposal of the villagers would be rocks thrown from above. Brogan wished that he had a few sticks of dynamite but, although he had not asked, he doubted if there was any in the village.

After surveying the gully from above for some time, he eventually descended into the gully itself where he looked up. Anyone above would be well hidden and already a plan was forming in his mind. Whether it would work or not was very much down to the villagers.

3

Before talking to the villagers, Brogan
and the village headman went to see
Padre Luis Salada. Brogan explained
his idea to both of them and was not at
all surprised when they both appeared
very doubtful.

'Rocks against guns?' muttered the
priest. 'I fear many deaths.'

'And you'll fear just as many deaths if
you stand around doin' nothin'', said
Brogan. 'You asked for my advice,
Padre; for what it's worth that's what
I've come up with. Have either of you
any better ideas?'

'No, Señor McNally,' said the old
man giving a deep sigh. 'It is just that
throwing stones would seem so futile.'

'And I have given the matter much
thought,' said the priest. 'I am a priest,
señor, my conscience will not permit
me to agree to anything which would

mean the death of anyone, not even Pablo Santos.'

'Then all I can say is go to hell in your own way,' snapped Brogan, losing patience. 'It wouldn't be as futile as you might think. That's a narrow gully and I can assure you that a rock thrown from that height can cause a lot of damage. Men can be seriously injured and even killed.'

'*Sí* Señor McNally,' said the priest. 'That is my point. I have seen a man killed by a single rock falling from that same gully. As a priest I must oppose any killing. We are not murderers and I cannot expect these people to turn into murderers.'

'*Murderers!*' Brogan shouted at them both. 'Since when did defendin' yourselves make you murderers? You asked for my help and you've heard what I have to say. Now if you don't like what I have to say or you don't want that help, just say so now an' I'll saddle my horse an' ride out of this damned place right now. If your conscience won't even allow you to kill in self-defence, I can assure you that mine *will* allow me to leave everyone in this village to whatever fate Santos chooses to deal out. Do I make myself clear?'

The old man placed his hand on Brogan's arm and smiled weakly.

'Please, Señor McNally, do not leave us now. Of course Padre Luis must stand against murder, as do we all, but I agree with you that it would not be murder if it is necessary to kill in order to defend our women and children. Perhaps, padre, you will explain to the children why it is they must die? If there is no other way then we must kill. Don't you see, Padre, that Señor McNally is quite right. Does not the Bible say that it is permissible to take an eye for an eye?'

'In the Old Testament,' agreed the priest. 'It does not say so in the New Testament, which is the word of our Lord Jesus.'

'I am sorry that your conscience will not see it as Señor McNally and I do,

Padre,' said the old man. 'There will be a meeting of the entire village very soon. We shall put it to the vote. If they agree with you, so be it, Señor McNally will leave us to our fate. If they agree with his plan then we must leave you to wrestle with your own conscience, Padre.'

'An' while you're strugglin' with your conscience, Padre,' said Brogan, 'ask it how it would feel if, by doing nothing at all, Pablo Santos kills all these people or even one more of them. Like he says, ask your conscience to explain it to the children. Your conscience might be clear but everybody in this village will be very dead an' they will all have died for the sake of one man's conscience — yours!'

'Unfortunately, you are both right,' sighed the priest. 'Very well, but it is with a heavy heart that I agree. We shall consult the villagers.'

The reaction of the villagers to the idea was, rather predictably, somewhat mixed. However, they were all agreed that they simply could not stand by and allow Santos to do as he pleased. Eventually, and after a tirade in favour from the mother of the boy Brogan had saved, all agreed to the plan.

That night passed without incident and Brogan was up and about at first light, intent on making his preparations. However, he did not get very far; a sudden call went up in the village that the army were approaching. He had to admit to being quite surprised at the efficiency of their unseen telegraph system. In this case it turned out to be a small boy who had been sent to a nearby hill to keep watch.

A short time later a troop of about thirty soldiers rode into the village but by that time almost everybody had taken refuge in their homes. They appeared just as terrified of the soldiers as they did of Pablo Santos.

From past experience Brogan knew why they should be so frightened. Mexican soldiers were not above helping themselves to the women and anything else in small, remote villages such as Santa Cruz. The only people to greet the soldiers were Padre Luis Salada and the village headman. Brogan remained in the back-ground.

After a brief conversation in Spanish between the priest and the officer in charge of the soldiers, the officer glared at Brogan and motioned him forward.

'What are you doing here?' demanded the officer.

'I like it here in Mexico,' said Brogan. 'I make a point of coming here whenever I can.'

'You are *Americano?*' asked the officer. 'Do you not like your own country? I do not think you come here because you like Mexico, I think you come to look for the money.'

'What money?' asked Brogan.

'You must know very well what money,' snapped the officer. 'It has become common knowledge. I find it very strange that an *Americano* should arrive at the same time.'

'All I know is what these people tell

me,' said Brogan. 'They've looked everywhere and so have I, I admit that, but it just ain't here.'

'And never was here,' said the officer with a sarcastic laugh. 'It was rumoured that three men stole the money across the border and hid it in Santa Cruz. We caught one of those men and sent him to prison. Unfortunately for him it was the same prison where Pablo Santos was also detained. I have heard that Santos beat the man to death before he escaped.'

'And you are looking for Santos,' said Brogan, not so much as a question but as a statement.

'*Sí*, we search for Pablo Santos,' said the officer.

'Well he's around here somewhere,' said Brogan. 'He was in the village yesterday. It seems I got here just in time as well, I stopped him hangin' one of their boys.'

'*You* stopped him!' exclaimed the officer. 'How is it that you are still alive? I know Santos does not like *Americanos*. He always kills those he finds, but that is not the reason we look for him. We look for him because he killed two of the guards when he escaped. You have been very lucky so far, *señor* . . . .' He looked questioningly at Brogan.

'McNally,' said Brogan. 'Brogan McNally.'

'Señor Brogan McNally,' repeated the officer. 'You have been very lucky, Señor McNally, I suggest that you remain lucky by leaving Mexico as soon as possible. Pablo Santos will try to kill you if you stay here. I shall not shed any tears if he does kill you.'

'I'll think about it,' said Brogan. 'Right now I'm more interested in what happens to these people. They know nothin' about any money but Santos doesn't believe them. I think you ought to protect this village.'

'They know nothing because there is no money,' said the officer. 'And I resent you trying to tell me what I should do. I have neither the men nor the time to protect every village from *bandidos* and personally I do not care what happens to them. They are only worthless peons.'

'They're still people,' said Brogan. 'Anyhow, what makes you so certain that the money ain't here?'

'Because the American we arrested had almost fifty thousand American dollars on his person,' said the officer.

'But I heard there was somethin' like a hundred thousand dollars stolen,' said Brogan.

'That is what we heard also,' agreed the officer. 'I ask myself what happened to the rest of the money and I ask this *Americano*. His answer was that fifty thousand was all there was. I also ask myself why he should hide some of it and I can find no answer. My superiors made enquiries about the money and there is strong rumour that certain of your people escorting the money used the robbery to cover up the fact that they had already taken the other fifty thousand. I am satisfied that fifty thousand was all that was actually taken.'

'That would explain a few things,' admitted Brogan. 'It wouldn't explain why he didn't tell all this to Santos though. OK, if there is no money, why not protect these people from Santos?'

'When I catch Santos they will be protected,' said the officer, dismissively.

'And in the meantime he's free to come an' go an' kill as many of them as he chooses,' said Brogan.

'That is how things are,' shrugged the officer. 'Now, my men are hungry, they have not eaten since yesterday afternoon.' He turned to the old man. 'You will provide food and drink.'

'*Sí*, Excellency,' muttered the old man. 'We do not have much but you are most welcome to that which we do have.'

'When we have eaten we shall talk of Pablo Santos,' said the officer. 'Do you speak Spanish, Señor McNally?'

'A few words, that's all,' said Brogan. 'Why do you ask?'

'Because you interest me, *señor*,' said the officer. 'Any man who can survive or get the better of Pablo Santos interests me. I shall send for you.'

The officer barked an order at his men and they all went off towards the cantina. The common soldiers remained outside, sitting on the ground, whilst the officer and two sergeants went inside. The old man followed and fussed around as his wife served what food she had. It was plainly not enough and she was dispatched to all the other houses in the village. Eventually women were crossing the square bearing what little food they had.

'So that hundred thousand has now become either nothing or only fifty thousand,' Brogan said to Padre Salada. 'At least they don't seem interested in your women. Or does that come later?'

'There is no way of knowing,' said the priest. 'They do not kill our men but I fear for the women. I agree that so far they have not done anything, but it might only be a matter of time before they do. I have seen it before, Señor McNally. They have no regard for the peons. I have seen every woman and girl raped by soldiers before now. Not here, but in other villages.'

'Did you tell the authorities about it?' asked Brogan.

'*Sí*, they were informed,' said the priest, 'but I was laughed at and told that peons were unimportant. There is nothing we can do to stop them. Sometimes the villagers fear the military far more than the *bandidos*. Sometimes it is with good reason.'

'I know exactly what you mean,' said Brogan. 'I suppose the only saving grace of having them here is that Santos won't come anywhere near.'

'We must be thankful for small mercies,' sighed the priest.

The sudden scream of a woman serving food to the men outside the cantina had all the other soldiers laughing. One of them was dragging the woman to the ground and his intentions appeared obvious. Without thinking Brogan ran across the square, gun in hand.

'Leave her alone!' he ordered, pointing his gun at the soldier.

The soldier stopped what he was doing and looked up at Brogan in surprise. Very slowly an almost toothless smile spread across his face as he stood up, picked up his rifle and aimed at Brogan's chest. Brogan saw that several other soldiers had also aimed their rifles at him. He feared the worst.

'That was very foolish of you, Señor McNally,' said the officer as he emerged from the cantina. He spoke to the men in Spanish and they very reluctantly lowered their rifles. 'You are most fortunate that I came to see what the scream was. I would not normally bother about them taking the woman, it has been many days since they had the chance. Also I would not normally bother about them killing such as you but what you have just done makes you even more interesting. Come, we shall talk.'

'Tell your men to leave the women alone,' said Brogan, replacing his pistol.

'And if they do not, señor?' asked the officer with a wry smile. 'Will you kill all thirty-one of us?'

'If I have to,' said Brogan with a certain amount of arrogance.

'And I do believe that you would try,' said the officer. 'You are indeed a very interesting man. We will talk in the cantina.' He barked an order at his men in Spanish and they all glowered at Brogan, but the woman was allowed to go free.

'Please sit down, señor,' invited the officer, indicating a rough bench. 'Perhaps you would like a drink? I do not know what this filthy stuff is but it is all they have. They do not even have any coffee.' Brogan declined and waited for the officer to continue. 'You obviously have no fear,' continued the officer. 'Either that or you are completely loco. I choose to believe that you have no fear. I could easily have allowed my men to kill you out there and I do not think that anyone would have been any the wiser. Is that how you tackled Pablo Santos?'

'Not quite,' admitted Brogan. 'What I did just now was somethin' purely instinctive. I was doin' it before I even realized. I guess I was lucky you were around. I'd probably be dead by now.'

'Be assured that next time I will do nothing to stop them,' warned the officer. 'I have been to America, Señor McNally, I have family in Texas, a cousin. I have also seen men like you before, men who do not live anywhere, who simply wander, stealing what they need. I think they are what you call saddle tramps.'

'That's what they say,' said Brogan. 'There's just one difference between me an' most of the others though, I don't steal nothin' from nobody.'

'If you say so,' said the officer with a knowing smile. 'Somehow I believe what you say, I think you have honour, which is most unusual. Have you killed many men, señor? I think you have.'

'I done my share,' admitted Brogan.

65

'Only in self-defence or when they asked for it though.'

'And would you have killed that soldier out there?'

'Probably, if it was a case of him or me.'

'But there were many more guns aimed at you. Your death would have been a formality.'

'Well, I'll put it this way,' said Brogan. 'In that case somebody would have gone with me. Who knows, it might even have been you.'

'Indeed it might,' agreed the officer. 'You are not a young man, Señor McNally and I suspect that you have been a wandering man all your life. In that time you must have learned many things. That would seem obvious to me since you are still alive. I have heard of men like you, we even have a few of your kind here in Mexico. They are said to be able to follow fish through water, to see where a bird has flown, to smell when danger is near. They are said to be able to find food where there is no food. Is that not so, *señor?*'

'I ain't so sure about followin' fish through water,' said Brogan. 'I hate water except for drinkin', but yes, I reckon I can find food where most can't an' I can track any man anywhere an' there's somethin' in bein' able to smell danger. I can't quite smell it but I always know when it's there.'

'Then I think that you are just the man I need, Señor McNally,' said the officer. 'I have been trying to get a guide, a scout, for many weeks now but it would seem that there is none available. I am enlisting you to help me track down Pablo Santos.' He laughed lightly. 'I need someone who can do this. I have no such skills; myself and my men could not follow a skunk and nothing smells worse.'

'Do I have any choice in the matter?' asked Brogan.

'Short of returning back across the border, no,' said the officer. 'I suggest that you think of it as a way to help these people. You will be ridding the area of a *bandido* and they will be free to live in peace.'

'Does that include peace from your men?' asked Brogan.

'You drive a hard bargain, *señor*,' said the officer with a broad grin. 'Very well, I shall instruct my men that these people are to be left in peace.'

'Then it looks like you just hired yourself a scout,' said Brogan. 'When do I start?'

'In three days,' said the officer. 'Unfortunately I must return with my men to my headquarters. We need more ammunition and supplies. We cannot go after Santos with what little ammunition we have, we would soon use it. I shall return in three days and then we shall go after Santos. The question is, will you still be here when we come back? I hope so, Señor McNally. If not for your sake I hope so for the sake of these good people.'

'Nothin' like a bit of good old blackmail,' laughed Brogan. 'Don't worry, I'll be here. Unless Santos gets here before you do an' kills us all.'

'And if he does come,' said the officer, 'what will you do?'

'I'm workin' on it,' said Brogan.

'*Sí*, I think that you do,' said the officer. 'I only hope that you are still alive when I return.'

'Not half as much as I do,' said Brogan. 'Since you won't be back for three days, there is a good chance that Santos might attack the village. Can I ask a favour of you?'

'A favour, *señor*?' said the officer. 'If I can grant it I will consider it. What is it you want? If it is guns the answer must be no, but anything else I shall consider. I hope it is not guns.'

'Dynamite,' said Brogan. 'I see you've got a couple of pack horses. Do you have any explosives? There are no guns in the village except mine and we need to protect ourselves. A few sticks of dynamite would be a great help.'

'You are in luck, Señor McNally,' said the officer. 'I have four sticks of dynamite and some fuse. *Sí*, I think I can let you have them. Perhaps with luck you will have killed Santos when I return. It will certainly save me a lot of trouble.'

'I guess four sticks is better'n nothin',' said Brogan. 'If he does come, I'll do my best to either kill him or take him prisoner.'

The dynamite and fuse were handed to Brogan and the soldiers lounged around for about another hour before they were ordered to mount up. The officer waved to Brogan as they left.

'I see they gave you some dynamite,' said the priest. 'I can understand why you should use it, but my conscience is still troubling me.'

'Better a troubled conscience than a dead one,' said Brogan. 'Now I'd better go see just how I can make use of this stuff. I won't ask you to come with me, Padre, I'd hate to make your conscience worse. If this doesn't work it seems that I've been hired to track down Santos. They'll be back in three days.'

'I think that you mock me, Señor

McNally,' said the priest. 'I only hope that your plan works. If it does not, I do believe that you will be very good at finding Santos. Of the two ways I would prefer you to be leading the soldiers to Santos.'

'Because that would mean you wouldn't know what was goin' on an' wouldn't have to agree to anything which just might trouble that conscience of yours,' said Brogan with a wry laugh.

'Again you mock me, Señor McNally,' said the priest.

Brogan laughed and walked off towards the gully.

He climbed up and wandered along first one side and then the other, trying to work out the best place for the dynamite, a place where it would do the most damage to anyone below and cause the maximum confusion. Eventually he decided that two sticks, one either side of the gully, should be placed at the entrance and another two, again one either side, placed at the end.

He spent the next two hours digging small holes close enough to the edge of the gully where the explosion would bring down the most rock. With luck, even if the explosion did not kill or injure any of the *bandidos*, it would effectively seal them in, making it easier for men above to throw rocks down on them. It would also mean that he would be able to use his guns.

He had seen six other men with Santos, but he did not know if that was all there were. On returning to the village he asked both Padre Luis Salada and the village headman if they knew how many men Santos had.

'I think it is about fourteen, perhaps a few more,' said the priest. 'Apart from the first time, there have never been more than seven of them. Why do you ask? Does it matter how many there are? Even one man with a gun could wipe out this entire village.'

'I like to know what I'm up against,' said Brogan.

'I think the padre is right,' said the

headman. 'The first time I counted sixteen of them. Since then they do not all come. It would mean that even if we killed half of them, there would still be others.'

'That's a chance we'll have to take,' said Brogan. 'Does Santos always come with them?'

'No,' said the priest. 'It depends on what they come for.'

Brogan nodded and smiled to himself. 'I have this feelin' that the next time they come Santos will be with them,' he said. 'He'd hate to pass up a chance of killing me himself. With luck, Santos will be out of action which means that they would be leaderless. I don't think those left will hang about too long without Santos to tell them what to do.'

'I think that those remaining would try to kill us all,' said the headman. 'They will not simply ride away, Mexican *bandidos* are not like that. They enjoy killing people.'

'We'll have to wait an' see what

happens then, won't we?' said Brogan. 'I want you to come with me. Bring a couple of your best men with you. I want to show you just what I intend to do.'

The headman called four other men and they all followed Brogan to the gully. Brogan spent the next hour showing them where the dynamite was placed and then assigning each of the four men to be in charge of certain areas. The headman was to act as his interpreter.

'How many men have you got?' Brogan asked the headman.

'Including young men over fifteen years of age, about sixty,' said the headman. 'I think that we can include some of the women, at least those who do not have babies or small children. Already some of them have said that they wish to be included. I think we can gather about eighty people.'

'That should be more than enough,' said Brogan. 'Right, the next thing we need to do is get as many people as we can out here now and they can start piling stones. The last thing we want is to be running out of ammunition.'

The headman spoke to one of the others and he returned to the village. He returned a short time later leading most of the other men and a few women. The headman explained what Brogan wanted and very soon everybody was collecting stones and rocks and piling them close to the edge of the gully. By the time the sun started to set, Brogan was satisfied that they had gathered more than enough.

Although it was quite possible that Brogan could kill any men trapped in the gully, he felt that it was far better for the villagers to feel that it was they who had defended themselves. He would, of course, be on hand just in case things did not go according to plan.

That night there was an air almost of celebration in the village. Even now they were beginning to believe in themselves.

4

The following morning, two boys were dispatched to the top of hills from where they would be able to witness the approach of Pablo Santos. Each boy was to signal using a mirror and another boy was positioned on the roof of one of the houses at the far end of the village from where he could see any signal. The hills were far enough away to enable the villagers to reach the gully long before Santos could. All the villagers could do for the moment was to wait.

'It would appear that there is no money,' said the priest. He appeared rather sad at the thought. 'I do not believe that Santos does not think so and no matter what we say I do not think we will make him believe otherwise.'

'I know the man had fifty thousand

on him when he was caught,' said Brogan, 'but I don't go along with the idea that the rest of it was stolen by the men who escorted it. To my mind I think that the other fifty thousand *is* here somewhere. Just where the hell that might be though is anybody's guess.'

'Even fifty thousand is richness beyond the dreams of anyone in this village,' said the headman. 'But, it is stolen money and we can have no claim on it. Is that not so, Padre?'

'They seem pretty certain that there isn't any more,' said Brogan. 'If you should happen to find it, who would be any the wiser?'

'We would, Señor McNally,' replied the priest.

'You an' your conscience again?' asked Brogan. 'If they don't want it an' they ain't even lookin' for it, why hand it back? It seems nobody wants it. First though, you've got to find it.'

'Sí, Señor McNally,' sighed the headman. 'As you say, first we have to find it. Already we have searched everywhere.'

'Perhaps if we come out of all this alive we will search again,' said the priest. 'If we do find it, I shall ask God for guidance.'

'I hope he gives you the right answer,' said Brogan with a wry smile.

'He will,' assured the priest.

Their day-dreams about the money were suddenly interrupted by a shout from the boy on the roof. He pointed to the hills.

'Santos comes,' said the headman. 'We must take up our positions and pray to God that we are successful. If you do not wish to join us, padre, perhaps you will pray for us.'

'As Señor McNally is at great pains to point out,' said the priest, 'perhaps it would be better if God was given a little assistance. I shall come with you.'

Brogan was rather surprised but said nothing. By that time people were gathering in the square and looking at the three of them expectantly. Brogan

nodded to the headman who immediately shouted an order in Spanish.
Suddenly everyone was running towards
the gully.

'They should be here in ten minutes,'
said Padre Luis. 'It seems that everyone
has been given a job to do except me.
What would you wish of me, *señor*?'

'The choice is yours, Padre,' said
Brogan. 'I don't suppose you want to
risk actually killing anyone so why don't
you help a couple of the women gather
rocks? If you want to, of course, you
can join in.'

'It is possible that there could be
injuries,' said the priest. 'I shall attend
any who do get injured. I have a little
medical knowledge.'

'Good idea,' agreed Brogan. 'All I ask
is that once things start to happen you
keep well away an' don't try tellin'
anybody what to do. Leave that to me. I
do have some experience in things like
this.'

The villagers were split up into two
groups and clambered up each side of

the gulley where they spread along. When he was satisfied that everyone was in position, Brogan called across the gully to the headman who was in command there.

'Remember, let them ride about half-way into the gully before you set off both fuses. Tell your men not to do anythin' until the dynamite explodes and to keep well out of sight until it does. Tell them not to try any heroics, I don't want anyone injured if we can avoid it.'

Using Padre Luis as an interpreter, Brogan then ordered everyone on his side to lie flat and not to move until the first explosion.

It seemed a good deal longer than ten minutes before anything happened and Brogan was beginning to wonder if Santos had chosen to avoid the gully. However, Santos and his men suddenly appeared about fifty yards away.

Brogan had positioned himself along-side the first stick of dynamite and so that he could see the approach to the gully. Eventually he saw what must have been every one of the *bandidos* ride in. Brogan did not ignite the fuse straight away, but waited for them to reach about halfway. They appeared to be in no hurry and were laughing between themselves. They obviously did not seem to be expecting anything to happen.

He waited until the last man was about half-way down the gully before he lit the fuse. At the same time he saw that the headman had also lit the other fuse. He raised his hand — a prearranged signal — and the two fuses at the far end were also lit. He then scurried away to what he considered a safe distance from the dynamite and waited.

To his horror, nothing happened either on his side or on the opposite side. He had calculated the length of the fuse very carefully, or so he thought. The dynamite at the far end was set to explode about one minute after the first two. It was now at least a full minute since the explosions should have occured, but still nothing happened. Suddenly there was a single explosion from the far end of the gully.

Immediately the villagers were on their feet and rushing to the edge. They were obviously very excited and, as well as throwing rocks, were shouting abuse at the men below. Still there were no other explosions. Brogan cursed and ran to see what had happened to the dynamite.

It appeared that the fuse had burned well enough but, although he was quite certain that he had set the fuses correctly in each stick of dynamite, it was obvious that only one of the four had worked. Brogan looked down into the gully and saw that the *bandidos* were milling around trying to control their horses which had been frightened by the explosion. They were now shooting at the villagers as he heard Santos barking orders. What he was telling them he had no idea, but few appeared to be taking much heed of him.

Suddenly they were racing for all they were worth back the way they had come, shooting at the top of the gully but without much effect. The villagers appeared to be following instructions and keeping out of sight except when they were hurling rocks. Brogan did not see any of the villagers injured.

The *bandidos* were now in an obvious state of panic and appeared intent on getting away as quickly as possible. Brogan saw two men fall from their horses as they fled, brought down by rocks hurled from above and, seeing a figure he took to be Pablo Santos, he raised his rifle and made no mistake in bringing the man down.

By that time there was no stopping the *bandidos*' retreat and in the absence of any blockage at the beginning of the gully, the villagers were powerless to prevent all but the three men brought down from escaping. The others were all very quickly beyond the range of Brogan's rifle.

For some time Brogan stood and

watched them disappear, silently cursing the unexpected turn of events. By that time several of the villagers had descended into the gully and were none too gently forcing the two men injured by rocks to their feet.

'Pablo Santos?' Brogan called, indicating the man he had shot. A man went to look. He turned him over and looked up at Brogan, shaking his head. Once again Brogan cursed. He had been quite certain that the man was Santos. He was joined by Padre Luis who, for once, appeared almost pleased.

'Damn stupid dynamite!' cursed Brogan. 'I should've expected it.'

'Expected what, Señor McNally?' asked the priest. 'That it would not work properly? I for one am not too surprised. I know a little about such things from the time before I became a priest. I worked for a mining company setting dynamite and I can tell you that Mexican dynamite is most unreliable. You have done your best and your idea was a good one, señor. It was most unfortunate that things did not happen as planned.'

'And I didn't kill Santos,' muttered Brogan. 'I could've sworn it was him.'

'I think that you killed his brother,' said the priest. 'They are much alike. If it is his brother, then I fear that Santos will seek revenge. He will now stop at nothing to kill everyone in this village. Santos and his brother were very close. They were both in prison together.'

'Well we caught two of 'em alive,' said Brogan. 'At least they can tell me where Santos is hiding. If nothing else I can tell the soldiers when they come back. I might even get out of tracking for them.'

'I think not,' said the priest. 'Santos is not a fool, he will know he has lost three men and he will know that you will question them. Even now I suspect that he heads for a different camp.'

'You're probably right,' sighed Brogan. 'I'll still question them though. Damn that dynamite! We had them exactly where we wanted 'em.'

'I think the only good to come out of this for the moment is that nobody from the village was hurt and that it will force Santos to think again,' said the priest. 'He does not know whether we have any more explosives. I think we shall not see him today.'

'Maybe so,' said Brogan, 'but when he does decide to come, he won't come through this gully again, that's for sure. OK, I'll go check why the other fuses didn't work. You get everybody back to the village and tell 'em not to be too severe on the injured men. I need to talk to them.'

An examination of the three unexploded sticks of dynamite showed no obvious reason as to why they had not detonated. All three fuses had burned their full length but the dynamite had simply not exploded. He was quite certain that he had connected each one correctly. He recovered the three sticks for possible later use, but he did not hold out too much hope.

When he returned to the village he

found the two injured men tied up under the tree in the village square. Somebody had made a point of throwing the rope used for hanging the youths over the branch above their heads with the noose dangling close to their faces.

Brogan's first thought was for the guns which the two men and the one dead man must have had and, rather reluctantly and after some insistence by Padre Luis, they were produced and handed to Brogan.

'At least we now have three rifles an' three pistols,' said Brogan. 'Take the gun belts and bandoleers off those men, that's all the ammunition we appear to have.' He called the village headman. 'How many of your men know how to handle guns like these?' he asked.

'Not many, if any,' admitted the headman. 'What few guns we possessed before were all shotguns. I do not remember anyone using a proper rifle or pistol before. Such things are very expensive, far too expensive for the likes of us.'

'Then the first thing to do is sort out which bullets fit which guns,' said Brogan. 'You can't use any old bullets, they could blow up in your face. Hand me them gunbelts an' bandoleers an' I'll sort 'em out. Then you can choose who you think might be best at learning how to use the guns. And remember, I want men who are not afraid to use them to kill if necessary.'

'*Sí*, Señor McNally,' said the headman. 'I think I know who will be most suitable. Six guns, do you want six men?'

'That's the general idea,' said Brogan.

The headman called out to six of the younger men, all of whom appeared quite proud at having been chosen. They stood around Brogan expectantly.

Brogan eventually sorted out which bullets fitted which guns. The three rifles presented no problem since they were all the same make but the three pistols were all different and of differing calibres. However, it did not take him too long to match each pistol with its correct bullets.

'Any of you speak English?' Brogan asked the young men.

'*Sí, señor*,' replied one of them. 'My father he taught me good. He say it good thing to speak English.'

'I'll agree with that,' said Brogan. 'OK, you can take charge of the others. I don't suppose any of you have ever used guns like these before?' The young man repeated the question to the others who all shook their heads. 'Three of you will have to learn how to use a rifle and the other three a pistol. Sort that out between yourselves.'

After a brief exchange of words the young man finally spoke. 'It is agreed that I shall take one rifle and these two the other rifles,' he said.

'Good,' said Brogan. 'Now watch closely. I'm goin' to show you how to load these things.'

Brogan spent the best part of an hour going through the procedure until he was reasonably happy with the young men. Loading the pistols presented few problems, it was the loading of the rifles which seemed to fox them.

'Now there ain't enough bullets to allow me to teach you how to actually shoot the things,' said Brogan. 'There's eighteen rounds apiece for the rifles an' just over twenty rounds apiece for the pistols. All I can do is give you a few pointers. Have all of you fired shotguns?' All of them nodded. 'Then it's basically the same. Just remember though, pistols in particular tend to pull up into the air. It might be better if you held them like this . . . ' He demonstrated how to use both hands to steady the pistols and then made each one go through the same procedure.

Eventually he decided that there was little more he could do for the young men and left them to practise. Each had donned either a gunbelt or a bandoleer and were now proudly strutting round the village, obviously trying to create an impression — particularly amongst the girls.

'It is sad to see them parading so,' sighed Padre Luis. 'Now they all dream of being the fastest gun there has ever been and of facing somebody like Santos and outshooting him. I fear that should they be faced with such a thing it is they who would be shot first. I shall be in the church should you want me.'

'No doubt about it,' agreed Brogan. 'I only hope it never comes to face-to-face shooting. Now to find out what our prisoners know.'

Whilst Brogan had been instructing the six young men, Padre Luis and his housekeeper had been cleaning the injuries to the two *bandidos*. Both had quite severe cuts, one to his head and the other to his shoulder. In fact it appeared quite possible, according to the priest, that the man's upper arm was broken. He could not confirm that it was but he seemed reasonably certain. The dead man had been laid out just inside the church.

Brogan had simply shrugged. There was nothing he could do or intended to do about it. He would leave any such decision to the army when they returned.

The two *bandidos* were sullen and at first refused to speak. The fact that Brogan could not speak Mexican seemed to make them even more determined to remain silent. Eventually Brogan gave a deep sigh, drew his pistol and toyed with it for a few moments while his questions were repeated by the village headman who was acting as interpreter. They still remained silent although plainly more apprehensive.

Brogan slowly placed his gun to the head of one of the men and told the headman to repeat the questions. There was silence again until he actually cocked the gun and pressed the barrel a little harder into the man's head. Quite suddenly there was a babble of information from the man.

'He says that Santos will not stay where they have been,' said the headman. 'This we expected. He says that there is a place further into the hills, to the south of where they were, which Santos favours. He believes he will move the men there.'

'How many men does Santos have?' demanded Brogan. The question was repeated and brought an immediate answer. The man also babbled incoherently, obviously pleading with Brogan.

'He says that the only men with Santos are those you saw.'

'The dead man,' said Brogan. 'Was he the brother of Pablo Santos?' Again the question was translated and the man nodded.

'Get him to tell you where the first camp was and where the new camp is likely to be,' said Brogan. 'It probably won't do much good but at least it'll be a start.'

A short time later the headman told Brogan that he now had a good idea where the original camp was and that he would explain to Brogan later.

By that time, however, several of the villagers, mainly the women, were beginning to crowd round. Brogan did not like their mood and spoke to the headman who in turn spoke to the women.

'They say that this one,' he pointed at the other prisoner, the one with the injured shoulder, 'was the man who hanged both Manuel and Jose and that they think he ought to hang as well. In fact they want to hang both of them.'

'I don't think so,' said Brogan. 'I want them alive to give to the soldiers. They might want to talk to them. I don't think they will be any more gentle with them though. I've seen Mexican army justice before.'

The headman translated and the crowd suddenly burst into a babble of complaints and general abuse of the men. Brogan listened for a short time before he suddenly stood up and shouted at them.

'No hanging, I said! The law will deal with them.'

Although he had spoken in English which most of them did not understand, it was obvious that his message got through to them. Still grumbling amongst themselves they began to move away, but not before several of the women had spat at both men. The *bandidos* seemed to realize that Brogan had saved them and smiled weakly at him.

'Think yourselves lucky, this time,' said Brogan. The headman translated and they nodded. 'I probably won't be able to stop them next time. Lock 'em away somewhere safe and keep a guard on 'em,' he said to the headman. 'I don't want them escaping and I don't want somebody sneakin' in an' killing them.'

'*Sí*, Señor McNally,' agreed the headman. 'I will instruct the men with guns to take turns guarding them. There is a small room at the back of the cantina which will be most suitable. The only way out is through the cantina.'

'I guess it'll have to do,' said Brogan. 'Now I'm goin' to talk to the padre.'

He gathered the three unexploded sticks of dynamite and went across to the church where he found the priest kneeling in front of the altar. He waited a short time before giving a cough to indicate that he was there.

'I knew you were there, Señor McNally,' said the priest, standing up. 'I was praying for guidance. What can I do for you?'

'First you can make it quite plain to the villagers that those two men are prisoners and that they are to be handed over to the army,' said Brogan. 'They were all for hangin' them both just now. In my book that *would* be murder, no matter what the justification.'

'*Sí*, I agree with you,' replied the priest. 'I shall tell them. What is the other thing?'

Brogan held out the three sticks of dynamite which the priest took and studied closely.

'You said you used to set dynamite charges,' said Brogan. 'Can you explain why these didn't detonate?'

'That was many years ago, Señor

McNally,' said the priest. 'I am certainly not an expert in such things. In fact it would appear that you have far greater knowledge than I do. If you are quite certain that the fuses were set correctly, then I can offer no explanation. I have already said that Mexican dynamite was most unreliable in those days and I do not expect that it has changed. I know that wherever possible American dynamite is used but I suspect that certain sections of the army are issued with this inferior explosive. It is very expensive and I know that the Mexican authorites will not scrap what they have. Even the army are given inferior weaponry, particularly in remote areas such as this, well away from the big cities.'

'OK, so it's bad stuff,' said Brogan. 'You must have had some which didn't explode. What did you do with it?'

'If it did not explode the first time then it is most unlikely it will do so again, at least not from a fuse,' said the priest. 'I have never done so myself, but I have seen such dynamite exploded by shooting at it. I do not think it works every time but I know that it does on occasion. It also means very accurate shooting.'

'I reckon I'm good enough to hit it,' said Brogan. 'OK, thanks Padre, I might be able to make use of it.'

That evening, food and drink suddenly appeared in the village and everyone appeared in very high spirits. It seemed that everyone felt that they had achieved a great victory and were determined to celebrate the fact. The festivities continued until quite late.

'I only hope that they do not celebrate too soon,' observed Padre Luis. 'Pablo Santos is not yet beaten.'

'Let them celebrate, Padre,' said Brogan. 'Like you say, Pablo Santos isn't beaten yet. I don't want to sound gloomy, but it just might be the last reason they *do* have to celebrate.'

'Let us hope not, Señor McNally,' sighed the priest. 'Let us hope not.'

5

Brogan sat bolt upright and listened intently; there were no obvious sounds but Brogan's senses were screaming that something was wrong and he never dismissed anything his senses told him. Quite what had woken him he did not know and, after listening for a time, he swung his legs off the bed and peered through the small window.

There was total blackness apart from a very faint hint of light above the distant mountains. Once again he listened and watched but whatever sound he had heard did not repeat itself. Nevertheless, he was quite convinced that everything was not as it should be. He picked up his rifle and went through into the cantina.

One of the youths appointed to guard the *bandidos* was stretched across the doorway to the small room where they were being kept. He was soundly asleep and Brogan did not want to wake him for the moment. He reached over and slowly eased open the door which opened inwards. He could make out two apparently sleeping forms on the floor and was satisfied that whatever had alerted him it had not been the *bandidos*. He gently closed the door and made for the main door.

He guessed that it was about four o'clock and the still night air was crisp with a hint of frost. Cold or even frosty nights were not uncommon even in areas which had normally very high daytime temperatures. He pulled his jacket collar up around his neck, and slowly stepped out on to the square.

All the time his keen eyes, well accustomed to seeing in the dark, watched for even the slightest of movements and his very sensitive hearing listened for the faintest of sounds. These senses had been honed almost to perfection over many years, years during which they had saved his life on more than one occasion. Even though he could detect neither movement nor sound, instinct still told him that something was very wrong. He moved to the solitary tree in the square and once again strained both eyes and ears.

Again, years of training and experience had taught him to differentiate between natural sounds and the unnatural. In the near distance the sound of an owl. In the far distance the sharp yap of a coyote followed by another coyote answering. These were natural sounds, sounds to be expected. On occasion though, even seemingly natural sounds served as a warning.

The briefest of snorts from a horse and the faintest thud of a hoof hitting the ground had him raising his rifle, ready for anything. Natural they might have been, but they were not in their natural place.

The sounds had not come from his horse which was in a nearby barn, nor from one of the few mules the villagers possessed; they had come from outside the village and from the direction of the gully.

Suddenly he heard muffled voices and just as suddenly the far end of the village was lit up by flares followed by a gruff command. Immediately came the thunder of many hoofs as horses galloped forward bearing burning torches, the flames seemingly hovering by themselves above the horses.

The riders were now screaming and shouting as loud as they could, the torches were thrown through windows and on top of the wooden roofs of the few barns and sheds. There was so much noise that Brogan was quite convinced none of them could hear him shooting.

He knew that he had hit at least three of the riders, although it was difficult to draw a good line on any of them. They were moving very fast and the light from the torches seemed only to serve to distort those figures he could see.

He was quite certain that one man

had fallen from his horse but the other two apparently held on and disappeared. He suddenly realized that the small barn which housed his horse was also ablaze. Rescuing his horse and saddle proved no easy matter but at that moment they were top of his list of priorities.

By that time most of the villagers had rushed out on to the square and the youths who had guns were shooting. Whether they knew what they were shooting at was very much open to question. However, it seemed that this time the *bandidos* did hear the shooting and, either taken by surprise or having achieved what they had set out to do, just as suddenly as they had appeared, they melted into the early morning blackness.

The intention had obviously been to burn down the village but although four houses, several wooden shacks and the barn were alight, they were now being dealt with and with remarkable efficiency. Padre Luis and the headman were directing the firefighters and in a very short space of time all the houses on fire were out. They did not bother with the purely wooden structures.

'We have found two bodies,' said the headman when things had settled down. 'They are both dead. We were most fortunate, the damage is slight apart from one house and there are no injuries or deaths among our people.'

'Glad to hear it,' said Brogan. 'I managed to get my horse out as well. I'd hate to have lost her, we've been together a long time now. We know each other very well an' sometimes I think she has more sense than I have. Two bodies, at least that gives us more guns. Have the guns and their belts brought over to me. I'll see to them when it gets light.'

'It is most unusual for *bandidos* to attack at night,' said the priest. 'I think that they must be very worried.'

'I've seen it before,' said Brogan. 'I wouldn't set too much store by it. The important thing is that Santos now has two fewer men. That should worry him more than anything.'

Two rifles, two pistols along with two bandoleers and two gunbelts were brought across to Brogan and, confident that there would be no further attack that night, he took them to his room.

The rifles turned out to be different from the other three they now had. These two were fairly old nine-shot revolving-cylinder Nichols & Childs, whilst the others had been makes he had never heard of. The pistols were E. Allen seven-shot. There were twenty-two rounds for each of the rifles and fifteen rounds each for the pistols. All in all, Brogan was now quite satisfied that they could withstand almost anything Pablo Santos cared to throw at them.

He was now well past sleep as were, it seemed, most of the villagers. At first light everybody was up and about, inspecting the damage that had been done. Apart from the very first house, which had been severely damaged, damage to other houses was relatively superficial and they all appeared structurally sound although they would need quite a lot of work on them to make them habitable again.

Obviously both the village headman and Padre Luis were very concerned as to the welfare of the family from the gutted house. The family consisted of a grandmother, mother and father and four children, all under the age of twelve years. The headman immediately mobilized most people in the village to clean out the house and to begin repairs. In the meantime the children were taken into care by the husband's brother.

Brogan, however, was rather more concerned with a further possible attack by Pablo Santos. He dispatched two boys to the top of two hills, sent one on to the roof of the gutted house to watch for their signal and eventually persuaded the headman to appoint four more men to take up arms. Once again he went through the procedure of demonstrating how to load and use the weapons.

'We'd better be ready for an attack,' Brogan said to the headman and Padre Luis. 'I've met men like Santos before an' once they get somethin' fixed in their minds nothin' will shift it. I'll organize the men. I've already got a good idea where they can be placed to best effect.'

'We are in your hands, Señor McNally,' said the priest.

'I thought you believed we were in God's hands,' said Brogan. 'What changed your mind?'

'I still believe that we are being guided by the Lord,' replied the priest. 'Who am I to question his ways?'

'Who indeed?' said Brogan with a wry smile. 'If Santos does attack, there could be injuries. Padre, I want you to organize the women into looking after anybody who is injured. Right now though, I've got work to do. We must assume that Santos is not far away and is liable to attack at any time.'

For some considerable time Brogan organized and placed his men. Those with rifles were positioned furthest away and so that they could shoot at the *bandidos* long before they reached the village. Those with handguns were placed in the village itself to deal with any *bandidos* who managed to get through.

Finding sufficient cover presented few problems, those with rifles being placed behind large boulders and those with handguns behind various buildings or other convenient hiding-places. One of the men with a rifle was placed in the small bell-tower. Brogan also had two wagons dragged to the narrowest point of the road into the village. Not that this barrier would present too much of a problem to any attacker, but it would make things just that little bit more difficult for them and mean there might be more time to allow Brogan to organize should it be necessary.

Eventually all the men were in position and all anyone could do now was wait for what Brogan considered the inevitable.

By midday, there was still no sign of Pablo Santos. Although this fact appeared to please almost everyone, Brogan was not too certain. Several times he called out to the boy on the roof who was watching for signals and each time the reply was in the negative.

'I don't like it,' he confided to the priest. 'I would have thought Santos would have attacked by now. I have me this feelin' that somethin's wrong.'

'What could be wrong?' asked the priest. 'It is plain to me that we have shown Santos that we are not to be taken lightly. Perhaps he has abandoned the idea.'

'Don't count on it,' said Brogan. 'Men like Santos don't give up that easy. No, Padre, my gut feelin' is that we've missed somethin' an' I never go against my feelin's. I can't for the life of me think what we have missed, but I know we've missed somethin'.'

'I think you do yourself a disservice,

Señor McNally,' said the priest. 'Because of you Santos now knows he can be beaten.'

'I don't think so,' said Brogan. 'Still, all we can do is sit it out an' hope.'

Suddenly the boy on the roof called out.

'He says there is a lone rider approaching,' said the priest. 'He carries a white cloth attached to his rifle.'

'Which means he wants to talk,' said Brogan. 'I can't think what the hell he wants to talk about but I guess the only way to find out is meet him. Instruct the men that they are not to shoot. I'll go an' meet him. Maybe you'd better come and act as an interpreter, I don't suppose it's Santos himself. He wouldn't risk it.'

Instructions were passed to all the men with guns that they were not to shoot and Brogan and the priest walked out to meet the lone *bandido*. When the man was about twenty feet away, he stopped and for a few moments he and

Brogan stared at each other as if expecting the other to try and shoot. Eventually the man lowered his rifle and removed the white cloth.

'I have a message from Pablo Santos,' called the man. 'He says that you are to give up this stupid attempt to defend yourselves. He does not want to kill anyone even though you have either killed or injured some of our men, but he will kill you all if you do not surrender.'

'No deal,' replied Brogan. 'We've now got enough firepower to deal with him an' he knows it.'

'*Sí*, this he knows,' called the *bandido*. 'However, what you do not know is that we have captured the boys you sent out to look for us. *Sí, señor*, I speak the truth. The two boys are named Hernando and Bernardo. Is that not so, Padre?'

'It is true,' the priest said, nodding sadly. 'We should never have sent them. I should have expected something like this.'

'It ain't your fault, Padre,' said Brogan. 'It was my idea. OK,' he called to the *bandido*, 'what does Santos want us to do?'

'It is quite simple, Señor McNally,' replied the *bandido*. 'You are to lay down all your weapons, including yours, and gather in the square outside the church. Do this and he promises that nobody from the village will be harmed.'

'But he doesn't promise that I won't be,' said Brogan.

'You are different, Señor McNally,' came the reply. 'Unfortunately I am not instructed to guarantee your safety.'

'Then why should I agree?' asked Brogan.

'Because if you do not, every man woman and child in Santa Cruz *will* be slaughtered,' replied the *bandido*. 'If the villagers agree they will be spared, as will the two boys we have.'

'First you must release those boys,' called the priest. 'They must be allowed to return before we agree to anything.'

'I am not instructed to bargain with you, Padre,' called the man. 'The choice is yours. The boys will be returned to you — one piece at a time — if you do not agree. You will also take Señor McNally prisoner. Santos will deal with him when he comes. That is all I have to say, Padre. Remember, the choice is yours, but remember also the fate of the two boys. Also you have prisoners, we are certain of that. One of them is the brother of Pablo Santos. You will now free those men and they will return with me.'

'We've only got two,' said Brogan. 'The others are dead, including the brother. You can have the bodies if you want.'

'That is a great pity,' said the *bandido*. 'Santos will not be very pleased that you have murdered his brother.'

'I'd hardly call it murder,' said Brogan. 'They just got in the way of a bullet, that's all.'

'I cannot agree to what you ask,' said

the priest. 'It cannot be my decision alone. I must talk with the villagers. It is they who must decide.'

'Again, it is a pity,' said the man. 'However, Santos is an understanding man and I am sure he will allow time for you to talk. I shall return this evening, at about five o'clock, but be warned that there is only one answer you can give. I am sure the villagers will do as you say, they have no choice if they wish to see those two boys alive again.'

He suddenly turned his horse and whipped it into a gallop. Both Padre Luis and Brogan watched him disappear. Eventually the priest sighed sadly.

'I fear that he is right, we have little choice,' he said. 'I cannot allow those two boys to die. We must surrender.'

'Part of the demand was that you also take me prisoner,' said Brogan. 'I'm afraid I can't allow that either.'

'You are free to go whenever you decide,' said the priest. 'My mind is quite clear, I cannot allow those two boys to die. I shall talk with the villagers but I am sure that they will feel the same as I do.'

'And if you do surrender and I'm not there, do you think Santos will be satisfied?' asked Brogan. 'He might still decide to shoot you all.'

'We are in God's hands,' said the priest. 'He says he will return at about five o'clock. If you are not here, we cannot promise to take you prisoner and hand you over. It is to be hoped that our surrender alone will be enough.'

'I doubt it, Padre, I doubt it,' said Brogan. 'I suggest we talk to the villagers and let them decide. Whatever they do decide though, I am not part of the deal, remember that. If you give up now, just when we have him wonderin' if we can beat him, I wash my hands of the whole thing, an' I don't wash that often, it ain't healthy. I know it's difficult for everyone, but I think you ought to make a stand of it.'

'These are not your people so it is

easy for you to say such a thing,' said the priest. 'No, Señor McNally, I think not. We cannot allow those boys to die. Believe me, Santos will kill them as easily as he would a cockroach. I promise that no attempt will be made to prevent you leaving, Señor McNally. I thank you for what you have done for us even if it has proved to be of no use. Your heart is in the right place. It is a pity that there are not more men such as you. Now we will talk to the villagers and whatever they decide, I must respect that decision even if it does mean those boys are killed.'

'Fair enough,' said Brogan. 'But be warned, Padre, should they decide that I must be handed over to Santos, there's goin' to be a few dead men about if they try, only this time it won't be Santos doin' the killin'. Those men might have guns but I doubt me that they will be able to kill me. I'm too good for that to happen even if I do say so myself.'

'Sí, Señor McNally, this I know,' said

the priest. 'You are a good man but also very good with a gun and can easily kill any of them. I think they also know this and they will do nothing to prevent you from leaving. They have too much respect for you to do anything like that.'

The villagers were called into the square and the position explained to them. Naturally enough, all but two or three of them agreed that they had no choice but to surrender. However, it was agreed without any dissenting voices that Brogan must be allowed to go free.

'We had no choice, Señor McNally,' said the headman, apologetically. 'We must now put our trust in God and the word of Pablo Santos.'

'Personally I don't think there's that much to choose between either of them,' said Brogan. 'I've yet to be convinced that the one can deliver and I'm quite certain the other breaks his promises all the time. He sure won't be very pleased if you don't hand me over to him.'

'His displeasure is something we must chance,' replied the headman. 'The decision has been taken, Señor McNally. I suggest that you leave as quickly as you can. For your own safety you must be well clear of the village before Santos arrives. Once again, on behalf of all the villagers, I thank you for your concern. We wish you safe passage to wherever you go.'

'OK,' sighed Brogan. 'If that's what you all want, then I reckon I'd better be on my way. I hope for your sakes that Santos does not blame you for me not bein' here, but somehow I doubt it.'

'It is not what any of us would wish, señor,' said the headman. 'Unfortunately it is something now beyond our control.'

Brogan saddled his horse, watched by a rather sad-looking crowd. The woman whose son he had saved suddenly rushed forward carrying a small bundle.

'Food, Señor McNally,' she said. 'It is not much but you are most welcome to it. I shall pray for you.'

'Don't waste your prayers on me,' advised Brogan. 'If you must pray, pray that Santos will not harm any of you or those boys.' He looked at the young men still wearing their bandoleers or gun belts and then spoke to the headman again. 'You've still got more than enough firepower to deal with Santos,' he said. 'You could make a stand.'

'*Sí*,' agreed the headman. 'We have guns. Unfortunately these men are not gunfighters, Santos and his men are. I think we would stand little chance against them. No, Señor McNally, we shall do as he instructs and lay down our weapons. It is the only way.'

'I hope you're right,' said Brogan. 'OK, I'll say *adios* and leave you to whatever fate you have decided on.'

He suddenly urged his horse into something of an unaccustomed gallop and rode out of the village. He did not look back, he very rarely did on such occasions. In fact he rode something over a mile before he did look back. He was at the top of a hill and now had a good view over the village.

'I guess you know what I'm thinkin', old girl,' he said to his horse as he patted her neck. 'I can't just ride out an' leave 'em.' His horse snorted and shook her head. 'Are you agreein' with me?' he asked. Again she shook her head. 'No? Sure, you're probably right,' he said again. 'It's their decision.'

He rode on but had not travelled more than half a mile before he suddenly stopped and spoke to his horse again. Talking to his horse was something he did regularly and just as regularly she seemed to disagree with whatever he said or decided.

'Sorry, old girl,' he apologized. 'I can't leave 'em. Them two boys are the key to it all. We're goin' to find where Santos is. The trail should be easy enough to follow. We should find where Santos is without too much bother, he ain't expectin' anybody to go lookin' for him, at least not until the army gets back. What happens when we do find him is anybody's guess, but I must try to get them boys.' Again his horse violently shook her head but this time Brogan ignored her.

He cut across the hills until he came out on to the clear trail left by Santos. However, he did not follow the trail, it was far too open and any look-out would have seen him long before he reached their camp. He made a careful note as to which way the signs pointed, left the main trail and headed amongst the many rocks which lined either side.

After about half an hour, he found a place where the ground was not so open and, after carefully checking that there were no look-outs, descended to make certain that he was still heading in the right direction. Having satisfied himself that he was still on course, he returned to higher ground. He repeated this operation three more times until he found himself faced with a narrow pass along which he was forced to go following the main track. The ground either side was far too steep to use higher ground.

As he travelled through the pass, his eyes and ears were looking and listening for the slightest of indications and sounds but, thankfully, all seemed very quiet. Twenty minutes after entering the pass he found himself at the end of it and looking down on to a small lake about a mile away.

Even at that distance he could see horses. There was no doubt in his mind that he had found the camp used by Santos. He rode slowly closer to the lake and the camp but stopped short about 400 yards away. He had been surprised that there was no look-out and assumed that Santos was very confident that he would not be found.

He pulled well off the track, tethered his horse to a bush and instructed her to keep quiet no matter what happened. This time she nodded her head in apparent agreement.

He made his way down the boulder-strewn slope to the lake and, finding a particularly convenient spot, settled down to study the comings and goings. In particular he was looking for the two boys. Eventually he saw one of them being ordered to draw water from the lake. They appeared to be being kept amongst a group of rocks and were guarded by only one man.

For some considerable length of time he watched and made mental notes, looking for possible ways to reach the boys without being seen.

6

There seemed to be only two possible ways to reach the boys and both involved circling the lake in one direction or the other. The way round to his right seemed to offer the best cover, but it would also bring him in to close proximity of the *bandidos*. The other way, to his left, offered less cover but had the advantage of keeping him away from the *bandidos*, apart from the last hundred yards. It was that last hundred yards which concerned him most.

The actual place where the boys were was amongst a group of fairly large boulders at the back of the main camp, such as it was. It seemed that everyone was open to the elements. Not that such a thing would have bothered Brogan, he had slept under the stars for the greater part of his life, but he had found that even hardened outlaws liked to have some sort of cover and comfort.

The boys were guarded by one man and it was quite evident that he did not take his duties too seriously. Often he would wander a few yards away and talk to one of the others and when he was not talking he sat in the shade and pulled his sombrero down over his eyes. He clearly treated his duties as something of a chore and probably thought it more a punishment than a duty. This boredom could probably be used to advantage by Brogan. The problem was how to get close enough to deal with the man without being seen.

He had been there about half an hour when Pablo Santos barked an order at one of the men. Brogan recognized this man as the one who had ridden to the village earlier that day. The man mounted his horse and Brogan had to assume that he was being sent to the village to deliver the final ultimatum.

His route from the lake appeared to

take him straight to where Brogan was now hidden but there was little he could do except try to keep well out of sight. Any attempt on his part to find better cover would more than likely have meant revealing himself. All he could do was keep still and hope. He was not too bothered that his horse would be seen, she was well hidden, but it was plain that the man was heading straight for him. He crouched low but at the same time keeping the man in view and he was ready to shoot if necessary.

About twenty yards from where Brogan was, the man suddenly turned to his right and disappeared behind a large boulder. He reappeared a few seconds later, this time more or less level with Brogan and had he looked to his left there was a good chance that he might have seen him. However, he seemed oblivious and continued along the track eventually disappearing from view. Brogan returned to the business of working out how to get to the boys.

He eventually decided that the best way to reach them would be to go to his right which, although bringing him close to the *bandidos*, offered the best cover. It would also mean that should he be seen, the inevitable gunfight would be to his advantage in that his targets would be that much closer.

He was almost arrogant in his self-belief, but that arrogance had not let him down yet. Out of nothing more than habit, he checked that both his Winchester and Colt were fully loaded, which they were.

It appeared that most of the *bandidos* were now intent on preparing their evening meal and all but the man guarding the boys and two others who apparently did not want to eat, gathered round the only fire, talking and laughing amongst themselves.

Brogan made his move; keeping as low as possible, he moved from boulder to boulder, checking regularly that he had not been seen. Not that he really needed this confirmation since had he been detected he knew that they would soon have let him know.

Making his way was a time-consuming business and on two occasions he had to cross quite wide gaps; had anyone happened to have been looking in his direction they would have seen him. On these occasions he had to wait until he was quite certain that nobody *was* looking his way before dashing swiftly but quietly across the gap. Again it was years of experience which enabled Brogan to move fast but quietly, almost sensing, without looking, where to place his feet.

Eventually these and other obstacles were overcome, although on one occasion he was quite convinced that one of the men must have seen him since he appeared to be looking straight at him as though he had seen something. However, the man's gaze was distracted and he returned to the matter of preparing his meal.

Once past the two wide gaps, the remainder of the distance was fairly easy and there was plenty of cover.

Eventually he was at the back of the camp and immediately above the spot where the boys were.

His main problem now was that there was quite a steep drop of about twenty feet between him and the boulders. It was not a sheer drop but steep enough to mean that he could well dislodge some of the loose stones on his way down, or he might easily slip and fall the rest of the way. It would also mean that for a few seconds he would be exposed to view to anyone who happened to look up. There was no real alternative to going straight down. Any other direction would bring him on to open ground and in full view of the *bandidos*.

The group of boulders themselves appeared to form a small cave and there seemed to be a gap at the rear which looked wide enough to enable Brogan to slip inside and for the boys to be brought out the same way. Before that, however, he had the little matter of negotiating the slope.

He awaited his opportunity and took it when a sudden loud roar of laughter went up from the men round the fire. He acted by pure instinct and literally jumped down on the basis that at least he would be quick and any noise he did make, even if heard, would be put down to rock movements and then ignored.

He landed more heavily and made more noise than he'd expected behind the boulders and for a few moments he held his breath and listened, half-expecting men to be rushing towards the cave. However, another roar of laughter from the men gathered round the fire told him that his descent had gone unnoticed.

He peered through the gap and saw that both boys were crouched at the small entrance, their backs towards him. He was about to attract their attention when there was a call from the men round the fire. The man guarding them grunted an order at the boys and both of them suddenly left the cave. Brogan cursed silently and carefully looked over the boulders, taking care that he could not be seen other than by pure chance.

It seemed that the boys and the guard had been summoned for some food. Actually this rather surprised Brogan, he would have expected the boys to be left to go hungry. It took the boys about five minutes to eat what they had been given and then they were given the task of taking all the dirty plates and the solitary battered cooking-pot to the lake and washing them. This operation took the boys about fifteen minutes and even then they did not return to the cave straightaway.

In fact it was about another ten minutes before they were ordered back to their cave. This time they were accompanied by another guard but it seemed that he too considered this duty as a chore and immediately sat hunched by the entrance, his back against one of the boulders, his sombrero pulled down over his face. Brogan allowed a few more minutes to pass before he attracted the attention of the boys.

This he did by a gentle 'psst' and, remarkably, the boys heard it first time. They seemed to recognize Brogan straightaway as he placed his finger to his lips as an instruction for them to remain silent, which they did.

To Brogan's consternation, the guard suddenly became very restless and stood up. He moved a few yards away and Brogan immediately took advantage of this and slipped inside the cave. It seemed that he had acted just in time as he saw, through the many gaps, that the guard had gone round the back where he proceeded to obey the call of nature and relieve himself. Brogan remained still and waited for the man to return.

Eventually the guard did return and suddenly peered inside. He saw the boys but not Brogan flattened against the side, seemed satisfied and immediately resumed his position hunched outside, his sombrero once again covering his eyes. Brogan once again signalled to the boys to remain quiet, drew his knife and moved forward.

He could see that the rest of the *bandidos* appeared to have their backs to him and, knowing that he might never get another opportunity, he suddenly reached under the guard's sombrero, cupped his chin and snapped back his head.

All this took a fraction of a second and the knife's sliding across and deep into the man's throat took another fraction of a second. Putting the man back into a sitting position with his sombrero pulled over his face as well, perhaps another five seconds. When he was completely satisfied that the others would think the guard to be sleeping, he moved back into the cave.

'Speak English?' whispered Brogan to the boys who appeared rather horrified at what they had just witnessed, though they had remained silent. Both shook their heads. 'Never mind,' continued

Brogan. 'I guess signs mean the same all over the world.'

He pointed to the gap at the back of the cave and made it plain that he wanted them to go through. At the same time he also made it very plain that they were to remain perfectly quiet. They seemed to grasp what he meant.

Once the boys were through and crouching behind the boulders, Brogan made a quick check that the dead guard was still in position and then followed the boys through the gap.

He realized that it was one thing for him to slip back unseen, but whether or not the boys could would be a different matter. All he could do was guide them and trust to luck.

Ascending the slope behind the boulders was out of the question. It was far too steep and stones would easily be dislodged. He looked about for another way and the only way appeared to be about ten yards away where there were a few large boulders which would give them some cover. However, getting to those boulders meant that they would be exposed for that ten yards, but there was no alternative.

He decided to go first and after making certain that nobody was looking in his direction, crouched and ran. He made it without being seen or heard. When he was in position, he checked again that nobody was looking and signalled the first boy to follow. To his horror, both boys ran across at the same time and a loose stone was dislodged. However, both of them made it and Brogan held his breath just in case somebody had heard the dislodged stone. It seemed that they had not. Brogan now indicated to the boys that they were to climb the ten feet or so to another large boulder whilst he waited, ready to shoot should it be necessary.

The boys seemed to know exactly what was required of them and moved with remarkable agility up to the boulder. When they were in position Brogan followed, hardly daring to look down as he climbed. He too made it without being seen.

From that point onwards, apart from the two gaps, the route back to where he had left his horse was fairly easy. They crossed the first of the gaps easily enough, but at the second it seemed that two of the *bandidos* were looking straight at the spot and they had to wait until the men turned their attention to something else. It was with some considerable relief that Brogan followed the boys across the gap and realized they had not been detected. From that point onwards it would be easy going, at least that is what Brogan thought.

He had not realized that reaching the boys and getting them back this far had taken so long but he was suddenly aware of the man sent to the village returning and at great speed. The man roared into the camp, calling for Santos, that much Brogan was able to understand.

There followed a lot of talking and pointing of arms and, although he could not understand what they were saying, he knew exactly what the man was telling Santos.

He was plainly telling his leader that he, Brogan, had left the village. This news obviously did not please Santos and he immediately ordered his men to mount their horses. He also called to the man outside the cave and, on receiving no reply, dispatched one of the men to wake him. The news that the man was dead and that the boys were missing had Santos and the other men drawing their guns and scanning the area.

Brogan ordered the boys to take cover whilst he took up position for what he now considered the inevitable shoot-out. Suddenly Santos called out.

'I know you are up there, Señor McNally,' he called. 'Those boys could not have murdered the guard. You would be well advised to surrender yourself and the boys. That way you may all live a little longer.'

Brogan remained quiet and motioned the boys to do the same.

'Very well,' Santos called again. 'We shall have to do this the hard way. It is a pity, think about the boys. By giving yourself up you have my word that they will not be harmed. However, if you do not, I cannot guarantee their safety. You are obviously a caring man, Señor McNally, I urge you, consider what will happen to those boys and the people of Santa Cruz.'

Again Brogan remained silent.

Santos spoke to his men, who all spread out and slowly edged their way towards where Brogan and the boys were hiding. It was almost as if Santos knew exactly where they were. He suddenly called out again, this time in Spanish and it was plain that he was addressing the boys. The boys looked questioningly at Brogan but, strangely, they did not seem too frightened. The boys looked at each other and then nodded to Brogan. He took this as a sign that they were not prepared to surrender.

Again Brogan remained completely

silent and watched and waited. It appeared that the *bandidos* were not over-anxious to venture too far. They obviously realized that they were fairly easy targets and therefore feared for their lives. Santos too sensed this and started to order his men but, with one exception, they chose to ignore him and slowly backed away.

The one man who had obeyed his orders slowly advanced and it was plain to Brogan that he would have little option but to kill him. However, not wishing to give his exact position away for the moment, he allowed the man to get right on top of them before his gun blasted away part of the man's face.

Immediately all the others started shooting, but none of them was prepared to venture any further. Even Santos held back. Their shots did not cause Brogan any problems.

The dead *bandido* had fallen between Brogan and the boys. Much to Brogan's surprise one of the boys grabbed the man's rifle and the other took his pistol. They indicated that they were ready to use them. Brogan smiled but was not too happy. He knew that whilst they might be very willing, they would stand no chance should Santos and his men attack.

By that time the shadows were beginning to lengthen as the sun slowly disappeared behind the mountains. This fact pleased Brogan. In the dark he and the boys would stand a far greater chance of escape.

It was also obvious to him that where he was now positioned, he would be able to shoot anyone who tried to leave the camp that way and, as far as he could see, there was no other real alternative route. He decided the best thing he could do was to keep them at bay until it was dark.

This fact did not seem lost on Santos, who had ordered several of his men to circle round and climb above Brogan, but he was quite satisfied that he would be able to see anyone and deal with them long before they could reach him. Nevertheless, at that moment he was willing the sun to set.

He had never really thought about it before, but it took far longer than he would have expected for the sun to disappear behind the mountains. Even so, it was still not dark enough to enable Brogan to risk making a dash for his horse. As the sun at last disappeared, Santos once again called out.

'I know what you do, Señor McNally,' he called. 'You use the darkness to return to the village. You waste your time, gringo, you will be found and killed, I promise you that. Not only do you now ensure your own death, you also condemn those good people of Santa Cruz to slaughter. *Sí*, I mean what I say. I will kill every man, woman, child and the priest. Before we do, however, the boy-children, the men and the priest will be forced to watch as my men enjoy themselves upon the bodies of their women, their sisters, daughters, granddaughters, wives and even grandmothers. *Sí*, Señor McNally, we shall defile every girl-child and all the women and then we shall kill them all. However, I am well known to be a reasonable man, everybody knows this. You can still prevent this massacre, Señor McNally. You can prevent it by giving yourself up now. I, Pablo Santos, promise that if you do, I will spare the people of Santa Cruz.'

Brogan was tempted to reply but decided against it. He had long since learned that men like Santos were very easily rattled by silence and it would be to his advantage to have Santos rattled. Men in such circumstances tended to act without thinking and make mistakes. As expected, his silence seemed to really annoy Santos and he tried ordering his men to attack. The men, however, were not prepared to put their lives at risk. Not for the moment, at least, and even those now circling the higher ground appeared prepared to go so far but no further.

Very slowly and far too slowly for Brogan's liking, the darkness closed in.

As soon as he judged it to be dark enough, Brogan urged the boys further up towards the narrow pass and to where he had left his horse.

It seemed that Santos had also judged it to be dark enough now and Brogan caught a glimpse, little more than a shadow, of him leading his men towards them. However, Santos had made one mistake, he was on foot and Brogan would soon be on his horse.

The fact that he would also be carrying the two boys would obviously slow him down, but at least he would have a reasonable start and would probably make it to the village before Santos. He hoped that he would be there in time to make the villagers take up their arms against Santos.

He found his horse without too much difficulty, mounted and pulled the boys up behind him. He did not waste any time trying to discover exactly where Santos and his men were and forced his old horse into an unaccustomed gallop along the narrow pass. For her part, his horse appeared to realize the importance of speed and galloped faster than he had seen her do in many a year.

By the time they were at the end of the pass, Brogan was convinced that he could hear the sound of horses behind and was even on the point of convincing himself that they were almost on top of them. However, he finally put this down to echoes.

The boy immediately behind him shouted in his ear, although he could not understand since it was in Spanish. The boy shouted again and Brogan chose to ignore him and thought that the waving of the boy's arm was a sign that Santos and his men were close behind. Suddenly the boy appeared to lose his patience and pulled at Brogan's hair. This time Brogan did take notice.

The boy was pointing off to his right and repeatedly flexing his arm in that direction. Brogan suddenly got the hint and realized that he was trying to tell him to go off in that direction. He nodded briefly, yelled something which was lost on the wind and swerved his horse to the right. This seemed to satisfy the boy.

They were now off the main trail and although Brogan had been forced to allow his horse to reduce her speed, they were still travelling quite fast. Being off the main trail, however, slowed them down even more and after a short time Brogan turned to the boy.

'Where the hell are you takin' us?' he demanded. The boy simply smiled, nodded and pointed ahead. 'OK, son, I only hope you know what you is doin'.' Brogan muttered.

The terrain rose sharply at first but at least Brogan now had some idea what the ground was like since, being high up, there was still some light from the horizon although the now distant and setting sun had disappeared.

Just as suddenly as the ground had risen, it descended just as quickly and it was then that Brogan realized that the boy had brought them across the hills and above the village. He could tell it was Santa Cruz by the few dim lights.

'Well done, boy,' he said. 'You probably saved us quite a bit of time.' The boy gave him a big grin and nodded as he brandished the rifle above his head. 'There's just one thing I ain't too certain about. What happened to them two prisoners?'

With this in mind, Brogan approached the village as quietly but as speedily as he could, eventually stopping short of the first building and ordering the boys, by means of signs, to lose themselves amongst the houses. He then led his horse behind the first house, took out his Colt and slowly peered round the corner.

The square was empty and everywhere was strangely silent, too silent for Brogan's liking. Once again his senses told him that all was not well in the village. There were dim lights in most of the houses and on the face of it all seemed normal. However, he was not convinced and slowly made his way towards the cantina. Once at the cantina, he flattened himself against the wall and, Colt at the ready, peered through the grimy window.

He had been right, all was not as it should be. He could just make out the forms of two men, whom he recognized as the two captured *bandidos*, sitting at the table and drinking. On the table were all the weapons the villagers had accumulated. He was not too surprised, plainly the villagers had released the men, who had then taken charge. There was no sign of any of the villagers. He moved quietly to the door, waited a few moments and then suddenly burst in.

There were four shots in rapid succession, followed by screaming from a woman which obviously came from the small room in which the prisoners had been kept. It only needed a quick glance to confirm that the two *bandidos* were dead and Brogan opened the door to the small room.

'You can come out now,' he said.

'They won't be no more trouble.'

'Señor McNally,' croaked the headman. 'You come back.'

'*Sí*, I come back,' confirmed Brogan. 'It's OK, the two boys are quite safe. They're probably at home with their parents right now.'

'The boys are safe?' asked another voice from the darkness. Brogan recognized this as Padre Luis Salada. 'Where is Santos?'

'Probably ridin' to the village right now,' said Brogan. 'Quickly, Padre, gather your men and give them these guns. We don't have any time to waste.'

'But what about Santos?' asked the priest.

'If you want to live, get your men together right now,' ordered Brogan. 'Less jawin' an' more action, it's the only chance you have. Take my word for it, Santos is in no mood to spare anyone.'

'I will get the men together,' said the headman. He ran out of the cantina.

'I fear that we will all be killed,' said

the priest. 'Why do you come back? It might have been better to leave us.'

'Probably you're right,' said Brogan. 'Fact is, though, I didn't so now you'd better make the best of things.'

A short time later guns, gunbelts and bandoleers were being handed out to the young men, who appeared very willing to defend themselves. The two boys he had rescued also appeared, both proudly carrying the guns they had acquired. Brogan was tempted to take the weapons off the boys but finally relented. There was no time to find other young men.

'You two just keep well out of sight,' he said. 'I didn't get you away from Santos just to see you killed.' The priest translated and the boys smiled and nodded before disappearing into the darkness.

'You are a very strange man, Señor McNally,' said the priest. 'What happens to us is no concern of yours. Why do you come back?'

'Let's just say I'm a stubborn old

man,' said Brogan. 'Now, I suggest that you get all the women and children into the church. They'll be safer there and it'll be easier to defend.'

'The Lord moves in mysterious ways,' sighed the priest. 'Who am I to question his ways?'

'Who indeed,' said Brogan. 'Now do as I say and get everybody inside the church.'

7

It was too dark for Brogan to see exactly where all the men with guns were, but the few he did find had taken up the positions he had previously allotted them, so he had to assume that the others had done the same. He also found his horse and led her to safety.

They did not have to wait long before Santos and his men suddenly rode into the village, obviously not expecting any opposition. Brogan had to assume that Santos thought that his men would still be in control. However, a barrage of shots soon told the *bandido* that they were not.

Whether or not any of the *bandidos* were injured, Brogan could not tell, but it seemed certain that none had been killed since there were no loose horses and no bodies to be seen. Certainly nobody fell from their horses either as they rode in or as they turned and raced out again.

Eventually Brogan became aware, even though he could not see them, that Santos and his men had taken up position some distance from the village. They obviously felt safe at that distance, Santos plainly knowing that neither Brogan nor the villagers dare risk an assault, especially in the dark. Suddenly and quite close, Santos called out.

'You are a very lucky man, Señor McNally,' called Santos. 'Sí, a very lucky man, at least so far. I do not know how you managed to get here so quickly or how you dealt with my men, but I can see that you have. That is a pity, they were good men but plainly not good enough to deal with you. You also have, what I think you gringos say, the devil himself looking after you. I mean no disrespect to the church, Padre, I too am a believer. We shall see how long the devil continues to protect you, Señor McNally.'

'Long enough to deal with you, Santos,' called Brogan. 'We've probably got more guns now than you have.'

'*Sí*, you are probably correct,' replied Santos, 'but I do not think any of those men in the village are very good with those guns. I have yet to meet a peon who is not frightened of guns or even his own shadow, and remember, I was a peon myself once. If it was just the peons I would have no problem, but I am certain that you alone are able to kill many of my men single handed. I wonder how good you would be face to face.'

'Just try me, Santos,' called Brogan.

'No, gringo,' said Santos. 'I am not so foolish as to think I can defeat you, at least not for the moment. I admit to not being very fast with a gun, I have never had the need. I am what you might call a careful man. As far as I am concerned, a bullet in the back kills just as easily as a bullet in the chest or head and is far less dangerous to me. No, I shall not face you. For the moment it is dark and you have the advantage. I can wait, gringo, I can wait. You cannot remain there forever. This is my country, it is not yours. You will want to get back to your own land soon, so I can wait. The only way you can protect the villagers is to take them back to America with you. I do not think this is possible. Do you?'

'If we must fight,' called Padre Luis, 'although I do not approve of killing, we would all rather die in our own homes. We shall remain here.'

'Then you will all most assuredly die,' called Santos.

'The army's due back soon,' said Brogan. 'Can you wait for them?'

'Perhaps they are, perhaps they are not,' said Santos. 'Even if they do come, they will not find me. They have tried many times to find me but have always failed. They are no better than peons when it comes to finding the men they chase. They too cannot remain in Santa Cruz for ever. Unless they turn the village into a permanent military base, they must leave sometime and when they do then I shall strike. I have time on my side, gringo, and time is a better companion than either God or the devil. Even should you escape me, which I now believe you are well able to do, the village will still be there. When the time is right I shall take great pleasure in allowing my men to indulge themselves upon the women and perhaps even the small boys before we slaughter everyone. Then every building, including the church, will be burned to the ground. Who knows, perhaps the villagers will be inside, still alive, as the buildings burn. Burning to death is quite a horrible way to die, Señor McNally. I have seen it. That is how my mother and father died at the hands of the soldiers. Perhaps you too have seen how people burn.'

'I've seen a few,' admitted Brogan.

'Then you know what it is like,' said Santos. 'Perhaps you will explain what happens to those stupid peons.'

'There's no money hidden here, you

know that, don't you?' called Brogan. 'It was all some story what got out of hand.'

'The money is no longer important,' said Santos. 'Perhaps it is there, perhaps it is not, I no longer care. I have been challenged and I do not refuse a challenge. All that matters now is that the villagers must be killed. They must be made an example to other peons that they can never beat Pablo Santos. They will become a warning to everyone else.'

'I thought you wanted me,' said Brogan.

'*Sí*,' called Santos. 'It would give me the greatest pleasure to witness you dying very slowly, perhaps even being burned at the stake or left to dry in the sun. *Sí*, that is a very slow way to die. The ants, they come from nowhere. They feed on your body and it is most painful. But I am no fool, Señor McNally, I now have first hand experience of you and know what you are capable of. Your slow and painful death would be my first choice, but I shall be happy if you are killed quickly. I also know that perhaps I can get none of these. You are a clever man, Señor McNally, sí, a very clever man and even though you are a gringo, I congratulate you. In fact I admit that I even admire you in a way. Should you escape me, I shall be sorry, but in other ways you are unimportant.'

'Maybe you'll find out just how unimportant I am,' called Brogan.

'Sí, you are unimportant,' replied Santos. 'You are as but a passing itch or fever, I shall recover. I advise you to leave Mexico while you still can. If you remain your importance to me will be even lower than a cockroach and I step on cockroaches without even knowing it sometimes. That is how important you will be. Now, gringo, we will talk no more, it achieves nothing. My men are tired. Do not think that you can find us and even if you do, what can you do? I would advise you to keep your men in position, you will never know if we will attack in the dark or not. *Adios*, gringo — for now.'

Brogan could hear the sound of horses moving away and eventually he could hear them no longer. Even so, he was wary and knew that they would not be too far away. He even toyed with the idea of following the *bandidos* but eventually discarded the idea as impractical.

'Do you think that they have given up?' asked the headman.

'I sure wouldn't bet on it,' said Brogan, 'but I think we're safe enough for now. Keep one or two men out on watch just in case though. He might come back. The rest can get some sleep.'

'I think that Santos is right, unfortunately,' said the headman. 'He can afford to wait. It can only be a matter of time before he strikes.'

'We'll see,' said Brogan. 'I'm goin' to get me some sleep as well. Tell the men you keep on watch that I am to be informed the moment they suspect anything, anything at all, even if it proves to be a false alarm. You can tell 'em it is just possible that they might try sneakin' in in the dark, although I doubt it, so they'd better keep awake.'

'*Si, señor*, I shall tell them. Sleep well.'

There were no calls made upon Brogan for the remainder of the night and, as was quite normal, Brogan slept well. Whatever his problems were, they rarely interfered with his ability to sleep.

He was awake and about just as dawn broke and immediately set to organizing the rest of the men. He even walked some distance from the village looking and listening but there was neither sight nor sound of the *bandidos*. He eventually returned to the cantina where he was given some food.

By that time, those villagers who had spent the night inside the church, were also up and about. Many even seemed quite cheerful and two women suddenly grasped his hands and thanked him profusely.

'They are the mothers of the two

boys Hernando and Bernardo,' explained the priest. 'They know that eventually Santos might come and kill them all, but they still thank you for saving their sons. Like me, they also ask why you do such a thing. Most people do not care what happens to peons.'

'I couldn't really do anythin' else,' said Brogan. 'Maybe I'm just stupid, but that's the way I am.'

'You are a good man, Señor McNally,' said the priest. 'It is a great pity that there are not more men such as you. You still puzzle me though. I know I have said this many times but, as those women say, what happens to us is really no concern of yours. Why do you do it? You place your own life in great danger.'

'On account of I'm a stupid old fool,' said Brogan, dismissively. 'If I knew the answer to that maybe I wouldn't bother. Mind you, it sure would make for a much easier life at times.'

'No, there is more to it than that,' asserted the priest. 'But I must accept that you are what you are and for the moment I am most grateful for it. Do you think that Santos will attack?'

'Again, if I knew the answer, maybe I wouldn't bother,' said Brogan. 'I'd probably be ridin' out right now if I had one lick of sense. Right now though we've got enough fire power to hold Santos off for a long time and he knows it. Like he says, he'll wait his moment.'

'*Sí*,' sighed the priest, 'for the moment that is so. But Santos is quite right, he has time on his side and time is not something you have. You must eventually leave us, that is your nature, and when you do, we shall be at his mercy. It is not now which is my concern, it is later, when you have left us.'

'Then we'll just have to hope that we settle this thing before I do leave,' said Brogan. 'I hate to leave a job half done. You're quite wrong about me not havin' time though. Time is the one thing I've had plenty of all my life. Sometimes I think I've had far too much time and not enough to do. Still, that's my problem, I chose to be a drifter.'

For the next two hours there was no sign of Santos but, as Brogan was making his rounds of the men positioned round the village, he felt a sense of unease. It was nothing more than that, just a feeling. He had seen nothing and heard nothing but the feeling persisted and Brogan, as ever, did not dismiss his feelings.

He instructed all the men, through the headman, to be ready for anything. He had no idea from which direction any attack might come, but he was now quite convinced that something was about to happen and he was not wrong.

Quite suddenly several shots echoed about and two of the men furthest away cried out in pain as bullets tore into them. He made a lightning-fast assessment of the situation and, realizing that any bullets fired from his side would be wasted, shouted for the other men to hold their fire. They appeared to understand without the aid of an interpreter.

Brogan studied the surrounding area and eventually located at least four *bandidos*. They were spread about and in good cover. However, they were close enough for most of his men to be within rifle range. He would have liked to have brought his men slightly closer to the village but could not since they would be exposed and in great danger. He left them where they were apart from ordering them to keep their heads down.

He managed to get to the injured men using a narrow drainage gully along which he crawled until he was close enough to work his way between large rocks. He discovered that one was hurt quite badly but the other had suffered nothing more than a slight injury to his upper arm. Despite bleeding quite badly, the man seemed quite certain that he would be able to carry on.

The man ripped part of his shirt and Brogan tied it round his arm. The other man was quite plainly not in any condition even to hold a gun and eventually he was dragged back along the drainage gully to the church where Padre Luis and one of the other women cleaned and dressed his wounds.

Much to Brogan's surprise, one of the older men took the man's rifle and bandoleer and announced, through Padre Luis, that he was ready to fight. Brogan did not argue but placed him closer to the village. This was not for his sake but simply because he felt that as the situation was, being closer to the village offered better protection for them all.

For the next hour the *bandidos* continued to shoot sporadically when-ever they thought they had a target, but by that time all the village men had taken better cover and were largely untroubled by the shots. The shooting was obviously designed to pin down the men in the village and to try and create panic to show them that it was Santos who was still in control.

During what appeared to be a period

of little activity, Brogan suddenly listened intently and summoned the headman.

'I think we got company,' he said to him. 'I don't think it's Santos either. Send somebody up on that roof.' He pointed to the burned-out building. 'Tell him to keep well down though.'

'How do you know this?' queried the headman. 'I can hear nothing.'

'Let's just say it ain't often I'm wrong,' said Brogan. 'Let's just hope it's the army. If it is them it should buy us more time.'

'Very well, *señor*,' agreed the headman. 'So far you have not been wrong. I shall go up on the roof myself.'

The headman climbed up on to the roof and was shot at for his trouble, but he was at the extreme range of most rifles and was not hit. Eventually he called down to Brogan.

'You are quite correct, Señor McNally,' he called. 'The army comes. The *bandidos* have also seen them and are now running away. Shall I send men after them? They do not appear to have horses.'

'No, let 'em run,' ordered Brogan. 'You can bet your life their horses aren't too far away.'

Five minutes later the same body of soldiers, led by the same officer as before, rode into the village. For the first time ever, as far as Brogan was concerned, the villagers appeared almost pleased to see the soldiers. Usually it was questionable who treated the peons the worst, *bandidos* or the military.

'Ah, Señor McNally,' greeted the officer. 'I was not sure if I would find you here but I am pleased that I do.' He looked at the village men who had been ordered back to the village and were now gathered in the square. He nodded slightly. 'I think you have been busy. When I left there were no guns in the village.'

'We've had a couple of skirmishes,' said Brogan. 'Nothin' we couldn't deal with. As a matter of fact you might have seen some of the *bandidos* runnin' away as you rode in.'

'*Sí*,' replied the officer, 'they were seen but I thought I had better come to the village first. How did you get the guns?'

'It's a long story,' said Brogan. 'Let's just say Santos doesn't have quite as many as he did before. That goes for his men as well. I ain't sure how many men he has left but I know he's got at least seven less than he used to have.'

'That is good,' said the officer. 'You are surprised to see me, no? I came back earlier than I expected.'

'Not surprised, just pleased to see you,' said Brogan. 'What's your next move? I presume you've talked things over with your senior officers. Mind, I don't suppose they give a damn what happens to any villagers.'

'You do me and them an injustice, Señor McNally,' said the officer. 'We are not as bad as you think. Tomorrow we shall search for Santos. You shall lead us to him. I hope you are as good at tracking as you claim.'

'I'm that good an' better,' boasted

Brogan. 'Why not go after him today? There's fresh tracks out there an' fresh tracks are easier to follow.'

'Because I do not choose to start today,' said the officer, grandly. 'The tracks will still be fresh in the morning. In the meantime my men shall eat.' He called out to the crowd in Spanish and, although rather downcast, most of the women trudged off to gather what little food they had.

Later, Brogan joined the officer in the cantina and explained what had happened in his absence. The officer seemed quite impressed.

'You are indeed a resourceful man, señor,' he said. 'It is a pity that you were unable to kill Santos. I am sorry the dynamite did not work properly but that is the way of things. I have learned not to rely on explosives of any kind. This camp where they held the boys, it is near here?'

'Not too far away,' said Brogan, 'but I doubt me you'll find Santos there now. He ain't that stupid.'

'But it will be a good place to start searching, no?'

'No, not particularly,' said Brogan. 'I prefer to follow the tracks left by the men you saw ridin' away.'

The officer shrugged. 'I am employing you to act as scout,' he said. 'It is your choice.'

'Employin'?' queried Brogan. 'Does that mean I'm gettin' paid?'

The officer laughed. 'I think not, Señor McNally. My English is not that good, it is the only way I can express myself. Consider it as your civic duty.'

'OK,' said Brogan, 'I get the idea. There's just one thing. I know for a fact that Santos is now down to about ten men, probably nine. I don't think it will need thirty or so of us to get him, half that number will be more'n enough. I want you to leave at least half your men in the village.'

'Why so?' queried the officer.

'Because he's threatened to slaughter everybody in Santa Cruz,' said Brogan. 'While we're away chasin' his tracks, there's nothin' to stop him doublin' back here an' doin' just that.'

'But the villagers are now armed,' the officer pointed out. 'They can look after themselves.'

'They might have guns but without some leadership they'd be lost,' said Brogan. 'It wouldn't take Santos long to rout 'em. Besides, I've always found it better if you don't go chargin' in with all guns blazin', so to speak. A few good men, well led, can achieve far more than a hundred men chasin' their tails.'

'And who is to lead these men?' asked the officer. 'I assume you mean that you shall be in charge.'

'That's up to you,' said Brogan. 'If I'm to scout for you, I also expect some say in what happens. It's my life too, remember.'

'I shall think about it, Señor McNally,' said the officer. 'Very few of my men speak English and those who do do not speak it very well. I do not think they will take too kindly to being given orders by a gringo.'

'Then you give the orders,' suggested Brogan. 'Just don't go off at half-cock spoilin' things, that's all.'

'Half-cock!' laughed the officer. 'That is a strange expression.'

'It means a gun goin' off before it's been properly primed an' cocked,' explained Brogan. 'When somethin' goes off at half-cock it tends to blow up in your face an' can do you more damage than who you're aimin' at. I guess what they call a flash in the pan is the same thing from the old musket days.'

'*Sí*, I understand its meaning,' said the officer. 'I must remind you that I am a trained and experienced officer. I come from a military family and I do not do things at half-cock, as you say.'

'I hope you don't take this personally,' said Brogan, 'but I've had dealin's with the Mexican military before and so far none of 'em has taken a blind bit of notice of anythin' I've had to say.'

The officer laughed and shook his head. 'I know exactly what you mean,

Señor McNally. I have had commanding officers who refuse to listen to what their junior officers have to say. Do not concern yourself. I admit that I do not know how to follow tracks, which is why I need you. I also admit that I have never been engaged in battle or a gunfight, at least not one of any real consequence. I sense that you are a very experienced gunfighter, very experienced indeed, but not as a soldier I think. I shall consider anything you have to say, any plan or idea and, if I cannot think of a better one, I shall follow what you say.'

'I guess I can't ask for fairer'n that,' said Brogan. 'Now, what about leavin' men here just in case Santos doubles back?'

'Very well,' agreed the officer. 'It shall be as you ask. I shall leave a sergeant and half the men here. We shall take the most experienced men with us.'

Brogan found Padre Luis and the headman and explained to them what was to happen next. Both appeared rather uncertain but, having little choice in the matter, reluctantly accepted it. Padre Luis seemed rather concerned that the soldiers who were left might take advantage of the situation and assault the women. Brogan promised to make certain that the officer impressed upon his men that the villagers were to be left in peace. This message was conveyed to the soldiers, most of whom seemed rather annoyed by the order.

With some time on his hands, Brogan walked out to where the *bandidos* had last been seen and examined their tracks. He soon found where they had left their horses and noted the direction they had ridden out.

Unless they had circled round later, the direction was due north, away from their camp alongside the lake. This Brogan had expected, but he did not know what lay due north so he returned to the village and consulted Padre Luis, the headman and the officer.

'It is dry and very hilly,' said the headman. 'There are a few waterholes but they are difficult to find unless you know where they are. I suspect that Santos knows the land very well.'

'I'd be surprised if he didn't,' said Brogan. 'The thing is they're goin' to need water wherever they go and so are we, so I reckon he'll be followin' any waterholes. Is there anyone in the village who knows 'em?'

'I must confess that I do not know the area all that well,' said the officer. 'Neither do my men. Most are from further south.'

'There is one man in the village who probably knows better than anybody,' said the headman. 'He originally came from a village close to the border and moved here when he married one of our girls. I believe his father was a hunter and that he used to go hunting with him as a boy.'

'Let's talk to him,' said Brogan. 'I like to know what I'm up against.'

The young man was sent for and, although he could speak no English, seemed quite certain that he knew where all the watering-places were. He was asked if he would go with Brogan and the soldiers to guide them if necessary. At first he appeared rather reluctant, claiming concern for his young wife and small son, but after the priest had taken him to one side, he eventually agreed. He also insisted that he be allowed to keep the rifle he had been given.

8

Shortly after dawn the following morning, with their guide riding one of the army pack-horses, Brogan once again picked up the tracks left by the *bandidos*. Eventually, and about five miles away, he came across where they had obviously made camp.

It seemed plain to Brogan that although they had camped there recently, they had not used it the previous night, the signs simply were not fresh enough for that. He very quickly picked up their tracks again and, much to his surprise, they continued to indicate that the *bandidos* were still heading north.

At about midday, they came across the first of the watering-holes. It was not very large, rather shallow and muddy-looking. Even Brogan, who was used to drinking the foulest of water at times, declined to drink it. However, its condition did not seem to bother the horses. The signs were that the *bandidos* had also rested there but there was no indication that they had camped overnight.

The officer also ordered that his soldiers should rest for a while and took the opportunity to quiz Brogan as to how far ahead he thought the *bandidos* were.

'At least a full day,' said Brogan. 'If we'd started out yesterday afternoon they'd be no more'n six or seven hours ahead.'

'My men needed the rest,' said the officer. 'We had travelled hard and fast to reach Santa Cruz as early as we could.'

'I guess that's somethin',' said Brogan. 'Still, I suppose it ain't none of my business how you go about capturin' outlaws, you're in charge. The guide tells me that the next waterhole is a clean one. We should reach it by sunset. We'll have to make camp there.'

'We are close to the border,' said the

officer. 'If Santos should cross into America, we cannot follow. I do not really know how far the border is, I have never been this far north before, except when I visited my cousin in Texas. In fact I should have asked for permission to come even this far.'

'Which would have taken another three days at least,' Brogan pointed out. 'They'd probably've said no as well. Even if they had agreed, Santos could have been anywhere in that time and the wind would have blown the dust and covered his tracks. They're difficult enough to follow even now.'

'I have faith in your abilities, Señor McNally,' said the officer. 'I wonder why Santos heads north? There is nothing out this way except the border. To the best of my knowledge there are no villages. I definitely know that there are no towns. I think it is nothing but desert. There does not appear to be any life at all.'

'It's desert all right,' said Brogan. 'If you know where to look though, there's a lot more life than you might expect. If there's nothin' out this way 'cept the border, then it looks like that's where he's headed but don't ask me why he should. As far as I know there's nothin' to stop anybody crossin' the border either way. I sure wasn't challenged an' never have been an' I've been comin' a few years now.'

'But it is not possible for the military of either side to cross,' said the officer. 'Even an accidental incursion into each other's territory can create a major diplomatic incident. We shall have to remain on our side and then we shall most certainly lose him. It is possible to arrange for the American army to look for him and return him to Mexico, but the process is long and is not always successful. Also, like us, they do not have the time and it is usually only for political reasons that criminals are apprehended by either side.'

'You might not be able to follow him

across the border,' said Brogan, 'but I'm an American citizen, there's nothin' to stop me.'

'There is also nothing to prevent you from riding on,' said the officer.

'True,' agreed Brogan. 'I guess you'll just have to wait an' see if I do or not.'

'You would try to find Santos?' asked the officer. 'Yes, Señor McNally, I believe that you would. Already you have shown that you care for the people of Santa Cruz. You could have left them at any time but since you did not, I do not believe that you will abandon them now. You are truly a strange man, Señor McNally.'

'Let's just say that's the way I am,' said Brogan. 'Stupid it might be, but I can't help that.'

That afternoon a strong wind swept across the arid land and, as Brogan was at pains to point out to the officer, the driven sand quickly obliterated any tracks left by Santos and his men. However, their guide appeared to know exactly where he was going and, just before sunset, led them up amongst a group of rocks where they discovered a fairly large, very clear and surprisingly cold pool.

Most of the soldiers took the opportunity to throw themselves, fully clothed, into the clear water to cool off and wash off some the dust which had covered them during the day. The nearest Brogan got to immersing himself in the water was to splash some on his face.

Brogan also scouted around the pool and the area immediately outside. He discovered unmistakable signs of the *bandidos* having spent the previous night there. At least it confirmed to him that they were now a full day behind Santos and that when he had started out that morning, he had struck out in a northerly direction. A short distance from the waterhole, the tracks were lost in the dust driven by the high wind that afternoon. All Brogan could do was to assume that Santos, for whatever reason, was still heading north.

The one person the officer had not brought with them was a cook. They normally carried at least one man who was able to cook, but he had been left behind in Santa Cruz, the one place where he was not really needed. However, their guide declared that he was a good cook and proved so to be when he made quite a passable meal of the maize, spicy beans, chilli and dried meat of questionable origins which was carried on the pack-horse he was riding. There was just about enough grazing around the pool and amongst the rocks for their horses. The many large boulders served as wind-breaks and it seemed that the wind was increasing in ferocity.

Brogan had many years' experience of desert winds and very rarely ventured out in such conditions. He had found it wisest, having found some shelter and a supply of water, to wait for the wind to subside. However, he did not make this point to the officer, preferring to wait and see what it would be like in the morning.

According to their guide, the next waterhole would not be reached until late afternoon the following day under normal conditions and involved the eventual crossing of a range of hills. The water was about halfway through the hills. He claimed that the hills were not very high but warned that the route through was steep and twisting and involved following the side of a couple of the hills along a narrow track with a sheer drop of about 200 hundred feet.

Such a thing did not bother Brogan, he had no fear of heights whatsoever but he could not help but wonder how the soldiers would react. Had they been American soldiers he knew that they would have dealt with it as a matter of normality. However, his experience of the Mexican military was one of their being not quite so capable and certainly less disciplined.

The wind was still strong the following morning but it was not strong enough for Brogan to insist that they remain by the pool. He did make the suggestion but was quickly informed that they could not afford to lose any more time in the pursuit of Pablo Santos.

There was no question and even less point in looking for tracks left by the *bandidos*, although the officer seemed to expect Brogan to be able to pick up their trail. All Brogan could do was to continue to lead them northwards.

They had been slowly making their way for about two hours when the wind suddenly increased in velocity and the sand drove into their clothes. The officer still refused to stop and for much of that time they could see no more than about twenty yards ahead as the sand and dust was whipped up. Most of the soldiers, including the officer, soon suffered from sore eyes and it was only Brogan, the guide and one or two of the older soldiers who had seen such conditions before who knew how to protect themselves.

On two occasions the officer seemed

convinced that Brogan was leading them in a totally different direction and even when his sergeant produced a compass and showed him that they were still heading north he was not too certain. However, Brogan did not use or need a compass, his sense of direction was very rarely, if ever, wrong.

By mid-afternoon the wind subsided and the driving sand settled. The guide, who could now see his surroundings clearly for the first time, announced that they had lost too much time and would not reach the hills before nightfall. He also said that as far as he knew there were no waterholes this side of the hills. Even so, the officer still insisted that they make as much headway as they could. He eventually agreed to call a halt just before sunset.

Without water there was no food since it was all of the dried variety. A few of the soldiers did agree to chew on some of the dried meat. Most took the opportunity to strip their clothes off, shake out the sand and rub down their bodies. Even Brogan stripped off, which was most unusual for him. He also told the officer to order his men to remove their saddles from their horses. He pointed out that the sand would have been driven under the saddles and would become a source of irritation to the animals.

As was quite normal out in the desert, the days were very hot and the nights were very cold, even down to freezing on occasion and Brogan had known of men freezing to death. Brogan was used to these conditions but it appeared that most of the soldiers were not. They did manage to find some brush and light fires, but there was not enough fuel to keep a fire going all night.

By the early morning the temperature had dropped dramatically but when the first rays of dawn broke, it seemed that nobody had died during the night. One or two appeared to have difficulty using their hands for a time but as the morning warmed up, so did their spirits.

'There's no way of tellin' how far ahead Santos is now,' Brogan said to the officer. 'We don't know if he was caught in that sandstorm or not. If he was, then we've lost no time, if he wasn't then I reckon we've lost another half-day at least.'

'And there are still no signs of him?' asked the officer.

'No chance, leastways not until we get to them hills. Maybe we'll find some tracks there, maybe we won't. The only thing we can hope for is that he was headin' the same way an' that's more'n likely since he needs to follow the waterholes just like we do.'

They reached the hills and the waterhole by mid-morning and the officer allowed time for his men to strip off, wash the sand from their bodies and in some cases from their clothes. Horses too were washed down and after almost two hours, they continued their search for Pablo Santos. It appeared that the sandstorm had also reached this point and if Santos had been there, any indications were lost beneath the drifting sand.

Half an hour later Brogan came across the first definite signs of men and horses having recently passed that way. There were distinct signs of hoofs having clambered up a large, flat, gently sloping rock. There was also a pile of horse-dung about half-way up. Right at the top edge of the rock, he found what appeared to be part of a broken spur and, judging by the fact that there were flies on it, what seemed to be blood on the rock. Brogan examined the blood and the piece of metal and decided that both were very recent.

From that point onwards and for the next three or four hours, the signs of men and horses were more frequent and, Brogan was now convinced, rather more recent than twenty-four hours old. In fact he was quite certain, going by the condition of the blood he had found, that they were no older than about six or seven hours. He did not tell the officer of his thoughts, but from that point onwards his senses were on full alert for possible ambush.

Although there were countless places where ambush would have been possible, nothing happened and that evening they found another waterhole. It was quite a large one and their guide was now able to cook. There were signs all around that Santos and his men had stopped at the waterhole, but it was apparent that they had not camped there. Once again the signs appeared rather too fresh to be anything more than about six or seven hours old. This time he did tell the officer.

'So you think we have made time of them?' said the officer. 'That is good. We will soon capture them.'

'Maybe,' said Brogan. 'What I would like to know is do *they* know we're behind 'em? I don't think it's a case of us makin' up time, they seem to have slowed down. There could be any number of reasons for that but we have to assume that they know we're followin' 'em. I suggest that you warn your men. We could easily ride into an ambush. That looks like ideal ambush country up ahead to me.'

'They would not dare to ambush us,' asserted the officer, 'we are trained soldiers and have much better weapons.'

'An' I reckon they're better trained in ambush techniques than you,' said Brogan. 'In the right place two men could take out this entire company. As for you havin' better weapons, don't count on it. We captured some pretty efficient firin' pieces at Santa Cruz. I sure hope they're better'n your dynamite though.'

At that moment the guide returned from amongst the boulders and spoke to the officer. The officer nodded and spoke to Brogan.

'It would appear that he has discovered a possible reason for them slowing down,' he said. 'He has found a shallow grave at the back of that large rock. He is quite certain that it is recently dug.'

'Let's take a look,' said Brogan. 'At

least it might mean one less *bandido* to deal with.'

The earth was scraped away from the rough grave to reveal a completely naked body. The guide explained that it was not at all unusual for bodies to be buried naked, especially away from the towns and villages. He said that all items of clothing, including underwear, were much needed and very expensive, which was why bodies were often buried naked.

Being naked, there was no way of saying that it was definitely a *bandido*, but he had apparently died from a bullet wound to his stomach which made it most likely that he was. The earth was thrown back over the body.

Brogan suddenly looked up and smiled. 'Buzzards,' he said. 'They can smell death from miles away. I reckon there's probably a few coyotes or foxes about as well. Another twenty-four hours and you'll never know a body was here. I reckon that's the way I'd like to go. I mean, my body won't be much use

191

to me so it might as well be some use to somethin'.'

'You are plainly not a religious man, Señor McNally,' said the officer. 'Most Mexicans believe that come Judgement Day, all men will rise again but only if they have a body. If there is no body then they are doomed to wander the earth in search of their body.'

'I guess I'll take that chance,' said Brogan. 'Anyhow, I got me a good few years' experience of wanderin' so it'll be just like home to me.'

They started out early the following morning and once again the signs were clear and fairly recent. At about midday they came across another pool of water and there were unmistakable signs that men had camped there the night.

Brogan had been alert for most of the morning and after this discovery his senses became even keener. Once again, he had an uneasy feeling although he did not inform the officer of this.

After a short rest, they continued to follow the signs and less than an hour later came to the first of the two narrow tracks round a large, rock-strewn hill. There was a steep drop, not quite sheer, of about 200 feet and Brogan's senses were now working overtime.

Before the soldiers started out along the narrow track, Brogan insisted on scouting ahead. He looked, listened and even sniffed the air but could not see or hear anything and that was his problem, not being able to see or hear *anything*. A close study of the rock-strewn hill did not show anything either.

'It's too quiet,' he said to the officer. 'In a place like this I would have expected birds if nothin' else, but there's no sign of even a buzzard an' that bothers me. It's also a good place for an ambush. Just take a look at all them rocks. You could hide almost the entire Mexican army up there.'

'Ambush, Señor McNally?' queried the officer. 'I think not. The track might be narrow and offer little in the way of cover for anyone using it but how can anybody ambush us? The valley is at least a hundred yards wide and anyone on the other side would be well out of range of most rifles. As for this side, yes, I can see why you think there might be an ambush, but no, I think you are quite wrong this time. I shall order my men to take the track in single file. I shall lead them. I suggest that you bring up the rear.'

Brogan chose not to argue and, as suggested, brought up the rear. It was his opinion that the officer had something to prove to his men and had used that moment to show that it was he who was in charge and not Brogan. This did not bother Brogan at all but what did bother him was the feeling that something was about to happen.

Brogan's original assessment of the abilities of the Mexican soldiers appeared to be correct. As they made their way in single file, it seemed that most of them were terrified of the narrow track and the steep drop. Their concentration was more on the immediate danger of falling than on the possibility of an ambush ahead. This also applied to the officer. In fact one of the few soldiers seemingly not affected, was the sergeant who brought up the rear and just ahead of Brogan.

The track took a sharp left-hand turn and seemed to go straight into the side of the hill before suddenly turning almost back on itself as it crossed a small stream. The officer and the first few men had just crossed the stream when suddenly a barrage of shots rang out, made to sound more than they actually were as the sound echoed round the valley.

Four soldiers behind the officer fell off their horses and one of them, apparently already dead, hurtled down the now sheer cliff and was dashed on the rocks far below. The officer leapt from his horse and hid behind a large boulder. More shots rang out, two more men fell from their horses but managed to remain on the track. The rest of the soldiers, now under the command of the sergeant, also dived behind whatever cover they could. Shots were returned but nobody seemed to know at what or at whom they were shooting.

There was absolutely nothing that Brogan could do and he turned his horse and returned as fast he could to better ground. Once there, he immediately leapt off his horse and, without giving the matter too much thought, scrambled up the hill.

Although the soldiers did not seem to know where their assailants were, Brogan had made a lightning assessment and placed the *bandidos* amongst a group of boulders which formed a line about fifty feet above the track.

He did not know, and at that moment did not care, whether he had been seen. His idea was to get above the *bandidos*. Judging by the shooting still going on he assumed that the *bandidos* were intent on killing all the soldiers. For the moment, this appeared to be working to his advantage.

The climb was steeper and higher than he had expected but eventually, with shots still echoing below, he was looking across a flat top about 200 yards wide. There was no sign of the *bandidos*' horses and he did not look for them. It seemed that his flight from the scene and his ascent of the hill had so far gone unnoticed.

He slowly made his way towards where he judged the *bandidos* to be and eventually found himself looking down on the line of boulders exactly where he had assumed they would be. He did not shoot at the first man he saw, instead taking his time and trying to place all of them. He had eventually placed eight men although he could not tell which one of them was Pablo Santos.

From where he was, he could also see most of the soldiers and it was more than evident that they were on the receiving end of what might easily become a bloody rout. Already it appeared that at least half of the soldiers had been injured and at least three seemed to be dead. Although they were attempting to return fire they were making no impression on the *bandidos*.

He carefully positioned himself where he could see most of the men and took aim.

His first two shots seemed to go unnoticed although he was quite certain that he had killed both men. As the second of his victims slumped lifelessly, one of the *bandidos* looked up and saw Brogan. Immediately he alerted the others and, apparently on an order given by Santos, all quickly sought other cover and concentrated their fire on Brogan.

Brogan's third shot again found its target, although he was not so certain that he had killed the man. A sudden, concentrated volley of shots forced Brogan to duck. When he looked up again, he saw three *bandidos* trying to make their way along the line of boulders. They seemed intent on escaping since nobody was attempting to get into a better position from which to fire on him. Another shot from Brogan and another *bandido* fell, this time appearing quite lifeless.

Quite suddenly and almost unexpectedly, complete silence descended. Brogan looked down but there was no sign of the remaining *bandidos*. He immediately ran off in the direction the *bandidos* had taken and found himself at the top of a cliff about fifty feet high. There was no easy way down and he did not try.

Suddenly and about 100 yards away, four horses burst out and raced away. The leading figure he recognized as Pablo Santos. There was little point in shooting at them and they were very quickly well beyond range. He returned to where he could see the soldiers and called out.

'It's OK, they've gone,' he shouted to the officer. 'I'm comin' back. Wait for me, I don't want anybody ridin' into another ambush.'

Ten minutes later he joined the soldiers who, by that time, were assembling their dead and injured. The dead, including the man who had fallen down the cliff, numbered eight and the more seriously injured added another three. The officer had escaped with a slight graze to his upper arm. The sergeant and the guide had not been injured at all. There were also three dead horses and another so badly injured that the officer had to order that it be shot.

'It seems that you were correct, Señor McNally,' said the officer. 'I am sorry that I doubted you. My one concern was to get to Santos. I made the mistake of assuming that I knew better than you.'

'I'm used to that,' said Brogan, rather cynically. 'It looks like it's left you with a problem though. There's only four of you left who are fit enough to fight. What are you goin' to do? I don't suppose you can just leave 'em here.'

'No, Señor McNally,' said the officer. 'I cannot leave them. I am sorry to say that on this occasion Pablo Santos seems to have won. I must return and report my failure to my superiors.'

'And no doubt you'll try to lay all the

blame on me,' said Brogan. 'Don't worry, I don't care. I mean, I'm a nobody and a gringo as well. I guess that should satisfy your superiors.'

'You do me an injustice,' objected the officer. 'If nothing else, I am an honourable man. I shall report that the decision to cross these hills was mine and mine alone. What will happen to me I do not know, but as a soldier I must accept whatever they decide. You will not be blamed, Señor McNally. As for you, what will you do now?'

'Go after Santos I guess,' said Brogan. 'There's only four of 'em now, so it shouldn't be too much of a problem. I think all except maybe one of the other *bandidos* are dead. Their horses are probably hidden not far round this hill. What are you goin' to do with 'em?'

'Nothing, Señor McNally,' replied the officer. 'Absolutely nothing at all. They will make good food for the buzzards and the coyotes.'

9

Brogan wasted no time leaving, he did not like farewells of any kind and he wanted to make up as much time as he could on Pablo Santos. When he did leave, he was greatly relieved to be on his own again. He had never enjoyed working with others, especially the military or the law of any country, although that did not happen too often.

As he left, the officer and the sergeant were organizing their dead and injured for the long trek back. The one man who had fallen down the cliff was left there since it was almost impossible to recover his body. The fact that he was nothing more than a common soldier was another reason in the eyes of the officer.

The guide informed him that the border was not very far and that he should reach it within three hours.

Having experienced many people's, and particularly Mexicans' ideas regarding time, he was not too convinced as to the accuracy of that statement, but it did not really matter.

When he had negotiated the narrow track around the hill, Brogan made his way to where he had seen the *bandidos* ride away. He found the remainder of their horses and, rather than leave them as they were, he removed their saddles and harnesses and turned them loose. There was nothing of interest to him among the gear they had left behind apart from a box of bullets which he could use in his own guns.

'At least you might stand some chance,' he said to the horses as he left them. 'It ain't your fault you was left behind.'

The tracks were clear and he followed them along the second of the narrow trails and eventually came out on to a dry plain. The tracks indicated that Santos was still heading north.

Exactly where the border was he had

no idea, but he sensed that it must be somewhere across the plain. In fact he soon discovered exactly where it was as he crossed a small river.

He had been riding along what was clearly the main trail even thought it was plainly not well used and, as he forded the river, a battered sign informed him that he was now in the Republic of Texas. He seemed to recall that it was not all that long ago since Texas had declared itself independent of Mexico. He was uncertain as to the present legal status of Texas but he did know that it was no longer a part of Mexico.

The tracks left by Santos still continued to indicate north, although they now turned slightly north-west and away from the main trail. They also seemed to indicate that Santos had slowed down slightly but he reasoned that that was probably because their horses were growing tired and not due to the fact that they now felt safer. Even so, Santos seemed to be maintaining a reasonable pace.

Brogan did not attempt to match the speed kept up by Santos, he preferred a more measured pace. This was mainly because he knew that his old horse, although very willing when she needed to be, could not keep up such a rate for too long. By nightfall he had still not seen any sign of the *bandidos* other than their tracks but he was not too worried, he knew he would find them sometime.

That night Brogan lived off the land, something he had done for the greater part of his life. He soon found himself a rattlesnake and a few edible bulbs. There was enough rough grass and shrubs for his horse and he cut some cactus for water for both him and his horse. Rattlesnake, other desert creatures and water from cactus were not his favourite food, but at least it was food. He lit a fire and was not too bothered about the glow being seen. That night was cold but he was well used to such conditions.

The following morning he once again picked up the tracks left by the *bandidos* and followed them until about midday. On the way he found where they had plainly camped for the night and was somewhat surprised to discover that they too had eaten rattlesnake and cactus. For some strange reason he had not expected men like Santos to know how to live off the land but there was obviously no real reason why Santos should not be able to fend for himself.

At about midday, he found himself at the top of a small ridge and looking down on what could easily have been a Mexican village, except that he knew he was now in Texas. He did not ride in, but took out his ancient spyglass and studied the small group of houses.

In fact they appeared not to be Mexicans but Apache Indians, which was to be expected. The main Indian populations in these parts were either Cherokee, Nez Percé or Apache. He also quickly discovered that Santos and his men were in the village.

He saw the unmistakable, smallish figure of the *bandido* talking to a group of Indians. He also remembered that Santos claimed to have Apache blood and wondered if these particular Apaches were related to him. One thing was quite certain, it would not be safe to simply ride in at that moment. The Indians would almost certainly take the side of Santos against him.

He found himself a sheltered spot overlooking the village, another rattlesnake and a large cactus plant. He cut some cactus for himself and his horse to chew on and waited to see what happened in the village.

Nothing in particular did happen for the remainder of that day. Santos and his men seemed to spend most of the time sleeping. Since there appeared to be little else to do but sleep, Brogan too spent his time alternately with his eyes shut and his hat pulled down over his eyes, and watching the village.

Even though he might have given the

impression of being asleep, Brogan's senses were, as ever, fully on the alert. Half-way through the afternoon he heard a slight sound and looked down to see a lone rider heading away from the village. His spyglass soon told him that it was not one of the *bandidos*. The rider soon disappeared from view as he headed westwards. Brogan did not trouble himself as to the reason for the departure of the man. He was quite certain that it had nothing at all to do with Santos.

Whilst he had been watching the village, Brogan had worked out that apart from the four *bandidos*, there were about fifteen other people living in five houses. At least two thirds of them seemed to be women, old men and a few children, which left about five who might prove to be difficult should he decide to take any action against Santos.

'I just wish I knew how long you intend stayin' there,' he muttered to himself. 'I can't wait up here too long.

A possible nine against one,' he sighed. 'I guess I've had worse odds but I'd prefer four against one. Anyhow, I ain't got no quarrel with the Indians.'

He also managed to work out in which house Santos and his men were staying, but to what use he might be able to put this information he had no idea as yet. Shortly before nightfall, Brogan lit a fire behind a large boulder, screening it from inquisitive eyes in the village. He cooked his meal of snake and a few bulbs and then doused the fire. Having no fire would mean that it would be cold during the night but, even hidden behind the boulder, the glow of the flames in the dark would be very easily seen by anyone below.

He toyed with the idea of going down into the village when it was dark and possibly taking out Santos but he eventually discarded this idea as impractical. Although he did not know the allegiance of the people in the village he very much doubted that they would be on his side. They were also innocent people as far as he was concerned and he did not want to risk unnecessary death or injury to any of them if he could avoid it. He would have to wait until the morning and hope for a better opportunity.

It was mid-morning before there was any real movement in the village, although many were up and about their daily chores from first light. That first real movement came in the form of Santos and his men saddling their horses.

Immediately Brogan saddled his horse and was ready for action. Eventually Santos led his men away from the village, at first heading straight for Brogan's position but then suddenly turning and following the course of a small river flowing southwest.

Tracking the *bandidos* from the ridge was, at first, fairly easy, but as the ridge ended and he was forced down on to flatter ground, it became more difficult to keep them in view without revealing himself. However, even though he appeared to have lost them a couple of times, he eventually saw them pulling up outside what seemed to be a farm or trading post. Whatever it was, it seemed to cater for the passing traveller, having two hitching rails, a large trough of water and rough wooden benches outside on the porch.

Brogan watched for a while and once he had established that the *bandidos* were the only people apart from the owner in the building, he decided to make his move. He was most certainly not going to get a better opportunity to take out Pablo Santos and his men.

This was one of the very few occasions in his life when Brogan felt that he could justify killing men in cold blood. He normally felt obliged to give his opponents some sort of warning but on this occasion he did not. The way they had treated the villagers of Santa Cruz was sufficient excuse for him.

The building seemed to be an old farmhouse which had been converted slightly and in fact it appeared that farming was still the prime function. There were cattle behind the farm and crops growing in fields surrounding it, but it was also apparent that the farmer had an eye for business and had turned the building into a saloon-cum-trading post.

The water trough was at the side of the building and, obviously unseen, he led his horse to it and allowed her to drink her fill. He too scooped a mouthful of the water as he listened, his ear close to the flimsy wooden sides of the building. He could hear muffled conversation and the occasional burst of laughter.

He checked his Colt largely through habit — it was nearly always fully loaded and ready for use — and, still with gun in hand, strolled casually round the corner and into the saloon.

Five startled faces looked up at him and there was a brief flash of recognition from Pablo Santos as the four *bandidos* went for their guns. It had been Brogan's intention to take out

Santos first, but he had been partially hidden by one of his men. However, four shots rang out in rapid succession and three of the *bandidos* collapsed on the floor.

There might have been no more than a second or two between Brogan's first shot and his fourth, but it was time enough for Santos to crash through a nearby window. It was also time enough for the owner to seize a rifle and aim at Brogan. A fifth shot from Brogan quickly disarmed the man as the rifle clattered to the floor from his now shattered hand. Brogan had deliberately not tried to kill the man.

Brogan raced outside, fully expecting to met by shots from Santos and he hurled himself behind an old wagon at the side of the building. To his surprise there were no shots. For a time he listened but everywhere was now strangely silent.

The building was behind Brogan and, quite unexpectedly, Pablo Santos, now on his horse, suddenly raced away.

Whether by accident or design, the building was kept between Brogan and Santos. By the time Brogan reached his horse the *bandido* was well beyond the range of his rifle. He was heading up into the hills and once again, knowing that his old horse would not be able to maintain any great speed, Brogan decided not to chase after him. He would, as before, be content to follow the tracks.

Following the tracks was easy enough, but nevertheless, Brogan was wary. Now that he had revealed that he was following the *bandido*, it was always possible that Santos might double back and attempt an ambush. However, by nightfall, and now well into the hills, he had not seen or heard any sign of the *bandido*.

He decided to rest for the night, although as far as he was concerned there was little to eat. He could probably have found something had he really looked, but going hungry for a day or two was nothing new. There was a small stream and plenty of grass which seemed to satisfy his horse and he contented himself with a drink from the stream.

He also lit a fire, not because he was particularly cold, but in order to advertise the fact that he was still there. He was hoping that Santos would see it and be tempted to try and take him out. However, it seemed that Santos had either not seen the fire or was not tempted, and the only real effect was that it did result in a sleepless night for Brogan.

As soon as it was light enough, Brogan once again picked up the tracks and an hour later discovered where Santos had also spent the night. About four hours later he came across what appeared to be an isolated homestead alongside a small river in a narrow valley.

He did not approach the homestead straightaway, his senses told him that Santos was not too far away and was quite possibly holed up in the house, although there was no sign of his horse. After studying the homestead for some time, he was almost relieved to have his feelings proved correct.

A woman, plainly of Mexican origin, came out of the door carrying a bucket and headed for the small river to draw water. Santos too made an appearance, his rifle held almost casually in his hand. As she scooped up the water, Santos looked in Brogan's direction.

'I know you are there, Señor McNally,' he suddenly called. 'Do not attempt to do anything. If you do the woman and her two small *bambinos* will all die. I am sure you would not like to see them die.'

'Ain't no bother to me,' called Brogan. 'If they die, so do you. I'm sure you don't want that either.'

'Why do you persist, *señor*?' called Santos. 'You are now back in your own country, you are free to go where you please. I do not know if you killed my men back there and I do not really care, it was their own fault. One of them at

216

least should have been able to shoot you. There is another thing. I know these hills almost as well as I know the hills of Mexico and you do not. You can follow me if you wish but you will never catch me and it is more than possible you will be killed. If not today, perhaps tomorrow or even in a month's time. As I said before, I have time on my side.'

'Time is the one thing I've got plenty of as well,' called Brogan. 'I'll trade you some of my time for some of yours.'

'Sí,' said Santos. 'I think it is something we both have in plenty. I must confess to a certain admiration for you, *señor*, even if you are a gringo, you do not give up easily. The only thing I do not understand is why you do it. I am nobody, the villagers of Santa Cruz are all nobodies and you too are a nobody. There will be none who will shed a tear should any of us die.'

'I guess you're right about that,' said Brogan. 'Let's just say that with me it's a matter of pride. I don't like to be beaten.'

'I too have my pride and I do not like to be beaten either,' said Santos. 'Perhaps we should both be content with calling things even between us. *Sí*, that would be the most honourable thing to do.'

'No deal, Santos,' said Brogan. 'That would leave you free to go back to Santa Cruz and kill them all. I ain't worked this hard just to let that happen.'

'Go back to Santa Cruz?' said Santos with a laugh. 'Remember, I have escaped from prison, I have killed a guard and I am now responsible for the deaths of many soldiers. I shall be the most wanted man in the whole of Mexico. *Sí*, I shall be a very important man. There will be a big reward for me. Everybody will now know and fear the name of Pablo Santos. Perhaps you know this and seek the reward, but I do not really believe so. You are a man who has little need for large amounts of money. I almost envy you for that. No, Señor McNally, for the moment at least, Mexico is the one place I do not want to be. Perhaps with time I may return, but your precious peons of Santa Cruz are safe from me for now.'

'I'd like to think they were safe from you for ever,' said Brogan. 'Anyhow, if I kill you I'd be doin' Mexico an' my own country a favour. Why should America or anywheres else have to put up with the likes of you?'

'I am not the only one,' called Santos. 'There are many more like me. Should you succeed in killing me, my place will be taken by someone else. That is the way things are.'

'That's a chance I'll have to take,' said Brogan. 'Just because there are more cockroaches don't mean I can't tread on one what gets in my way.'

'As you wish, Señor McNally,' said Santos, laughing. 'In the meantime I shall be warm and I shall eat good food. What will you do? The nights are very cold and apart from a few snakes and lizards, there is little food for you. I do not think this bothers you too much though. You are a drifter and well used to living off the land. The next move is up to you, gringo, I can wait.'

He laughed again and followed the woman inside the house but Brogan knew full well that either he or the woman would be keeping watch for any movement he tried to make.

He also had the feeling that the woman was not an unwilling prisoner and it was more than possible that she and Santos were far from being strangers to each other.

Brogan turned his attention to ways of reaching the house unseen and was eventually forced to concede that it was rather more difficult than at first appeared. In fact in daylight it would be almost impossible. However, Brogan was used to seemingly impossible odds.

Although the valley was quite narrow, the house was situated at what appeared to be the widest part. From where he now was, the approach was straightforward, there being about 400 yards of open ground. That was the problem, it was too open and there was virtually no cover between him and the house.

To his left the side of the hill rose suddenly and almost sheer, making it impossible for him to take his horse round. To his right and across the river, there was an area of flat land about 300 yards wide but this once again ended at almost sheer cliffs. Again, there was almost no cover.

Brogan also looked back to see if there was any way he could get to the other side of the house without being seen, but as far as he could tell and remember, the sides of the valley, although not that high, were very steep. Even if he did manage to get to the top, there was no way of knowing or telling where he would be able to get down again.

Brogan gave a resigned sigh and somewhat reluctantly decided that he had little alternative but to wait until sunset. In the dark he knew that he would be able to get much closer to the house, but he also knew that that would be exactly what Santos expected. For a few brief moments he even considered calling the whole vendetta off, for vendetta was what it had now truly become, but it *was* only for a few brief moments. In a way, he knew that he was simply being obstinate and that a large part of what he was now doing was down to little more than pride, but he was still resolved to ensure that the villagers of Santa Cruz would not be troubled by Santos at any time in the future.

During the day, his feelings that Santos and the woman were no strangers to each other appeared confirmed when Santos suddenly made an appearance in the company of two children, both boys. The eldest appeared to be about ten years old and the youngest about six years. The younger boy took the *bandido*'s hand in a seemingly natural manner.

'So you're a daddy,' Brogan said to himself. 'I guessed you might be. At least I now know whose side the woman is on an' it ain't mine. I'm almost sorry to have to do this to you, Mrs Santos — if that's who you are — but it looks like you is soon goin' to be a widow an' your kids orphans. Still, as your old man says, that's the way things are an' he made the rules, not me.'

Santos appeared to be taunting Brogan. He waved his hand in his direction and made the younger boy do the same. Later, Santos again emerged from the house, this time carrying a plate or bowl from which he made exaggerated motions of eating. Once again he was plainly taunting Brogan.

Such actions might have bothered other men, but it certainly did not trouble Brogan. It was in fact similar to tactics he himself employed when goading people. His reasons were usually that when men were goaded, they made mistakes. It appeared plain that Pablo Santos was attempting to goad Brogan into making a mistake.

Waiting for nightfall was, on this occasion, one of those occasions when time even seemed to conspire against him and pass deliberately slowly. This was far more galling than the rather juvenile antics of Pablo Santos as he attempted to goad him. Eventually however, the shadows on the ground began to lengthen as the sun slipped ever downwards to the western horizon. It disappeared from view behind the hills, although it was still light for some considerable length of time afterwards.

Before the light disappeared completely, Brogan had worked out his exact route to the house and had even allowed for Santos to be expecting him. His advantage was that even though the *bandido* obviously expected something, he did not know where, when or how. Brogan was aware that these facts alone would be sufficient to make the *bandido* nervous. When the light did at last disappear, he deliberately waited for another hour just to annoy Santos.

Eventually Brogan decided that it was time to make his move. Not unexpectedly, there was no light from the house, in fact nothing at all which Brogan could use as a guide. However, his years of experience of total darkness had honed his sight to such a degree that he could almost sense rather than actually see where things were. It did not take him long to locate exactly where he was as the shape of the building loomed up before him.

He pressed himself against the wooden sides and listened for any sounds from inside. There was none. He could not even detect the sound of the children breathing. This complete absence of sound was most unusual and it rather worried him.

Normally he would have been able to detect even the slightest intake of breath or the faintest sound of a foot being moved. He listened intently for some time and gradually became convinced that the building was empty. Just to be doubly certain, he moved to the door where once again he listened. Still there was no indication that anyone was inside the house. As far as he was concerned, it *was* completely empty.

Even so, it was with the greatest of caution that he lifted the wooden latch on the door and eased it open. He half-expected a volley of shots as the door swung open and he flattened himself against the wall at the side before slowly looking through the open doorway.

There was a very faint glow in the room which, he realized, came from the remains of the fire in the open grate. It was sufficient light for Brogan to be able to see exactly what was inside the single-roomed cabin. Apart from a few items of furniture, the place appeared to be completely empty. A quick check around the room soon confirmed that he was alone.

'Nice one, Santos,' Brogan muttered to himself. 'I've gotta admit I never heard you leave. The question now is where the hell are you? I can't track you tonight, that's for certain. Still, I reckon I can get myself some sleep.'

Just to confirm that the *bandido*, the woman and the children had left, he went outside and looked in the small barn. That too was completely empty and as he lit a match, the evidence was that at least two horses or mules had been in there but were now gone.

He recovered his own horse, installed her in the barn, found some feed and then returned to the house where he also found some bread, a piece of ancient but still edible cheese and a bucket of water.

10

Brogan was out looking for tracks as soon as the first rays of light were able to find their way into the valley. Finding them proved easy enough and, as he had thought, two animals had been used. One of them was obviously the horse belonging to Pablo Santos and the other, judging by the smaller hoof prints and the fact that it had no metal shoes, a mule. Not unexpectedly the tracks led up the valley since there was really no other way they could have gone.

He followed the trail for about an hour before the signs suddenly disappeared into the small river. At first it looked as though they had followed the water upstream but when he could find no evidence of their taking to either bank, Brogan returned to where the tracks had entered the water. It did not take him long to discover that Santos and the woman had turned downstream. He eventually located tracks leading from the river and up through a very narrow fissure between two hills.

His first reaction to the fissure was one of extreme caution. It was about fifteen feet wide and about the same in depth before broadening out slightly. His caution was because he realized it could well be an ideal place for an ambush. There was no other choice but to follow the fissure since there was no way he could get his horse on to the narrow ledge which appeared to run either side, but he was still taking no chances.

He left his horse at the entrance and climbed the sides. Even had he been able to get his horse on to the ledge, he could not have ridden far since it all but disappeared in several places. He followed the fissure for about half a mile before he was satisfied that Santos had ridden straight through. He returned to his horse and he too rode through. As ever, even though he was reasonably certain that he was not heading into an ambush, his senses worked continuously.

He eventually came out into another narrow valley and the indications were that Santos had headed north and all Brogan could do was to continue to follow. At the same time he was all too aware that the opportunity for ambush was ever-present and all his senses were still on full alert. He constantly scanned his surroundings and listened for the slightest of give-away sounds, but there were none.

Quite suddenly and most unexpectedly, as Brogan rounded a sharp bend, he was faced with a group of four rough mud-brick houses. Immediately he stopped and eased his horse behind a large boulder as he studied the dwellings. Once again they seemed to be occupied by Apache Indians. There was no sign of either Santos or the woman. However, wary as ever, Brogan studied the small community for some time before proceeding.

He was not too surprised when it seemed that the people were expecting him, although he was quite certain that he had not been seen. The only two men in the village seemed to be constantly looking in his direction even before he revealed himself. Eventually, satisfied that Santos was not there, Brogan remounted his horse and slowly made his way into the village. Again the feeling he picked up was one of being expected.

'I look for Pablo Santos,' Brogan said to one of the men, both of whom appeared to be very old. The man simply glared sullenly at him and did not speak. 'Pablo Santos,' repeated Brogan. 'You know Pablo Santos?' Again the man remained motionless and silent. 'Do you speak English?' he asked again.

In reply the man simply waved his arm, indicating down the valley and Brogan knew Indians well enough to know that he was not going to get any further information or help from them.

However, it did not escape his notice that there were at least three young women with children and he did not think that the two old men were the fathers of such young children. There were also two old women, the more likely partners to the two men.

He realized that there could be several perfectly good and logical reasons as to why there were no younger men to be seen, but instinct told him that it had something to do with Pablo Santos and his own arrival. He deliberately made great show of checking his Colt and his Winchester before moving on.

Whether or not it was his little act which produced some result, he would never know. As he left the village he glanced back just in time to see a young boy leaving and climbing the valley side.

Once out of sight, Brogan leapt off his horse and he too climbed the side of the valley and saw the boy standing on a large rock waving. The signal he had expected to be given had been given.

From where Brogan now was, he was able to see down into the village and once again he was not surprised to see the woman who had been with Santos and her two children emerge from one of the houses. Nobody seemed to notice that he was watching them.

A glance in the direction the boy had waved revealed that he was about to enter another valley which, though slightly wider than the one he was now in, appeared to be almost sheer-sided and strewn with large boulders. This was ideal ambush territory.

His problem now was how to wrest the advantage from Santos who was very possibly with some of the younger men from the village. In fact the only advantage he did have was that he knew Santos was expecting him.

From where he was, there was no sign of Santos or any Indians, but he was now quite certain that they were lying in wait. He returned to his horse and slowly rode on.

After a very short time he came to a point where the valley with the large boulders and the valley he was now in divided. He had been correct in his assessment of the valley, it was sheer-sided, rather more like a canyon. The trail and the few tracks he was able to detect invitingly indicated this wider, rock-strewn valley as the way to go but Brogan had other ideas.

It was not that he was afraid to face Santos or any number of other men, but he never knowingly placed himself in the line of fire. He had not survived as long as he had by taking unnecessary chances. He continued to follow the narrower of the two routes.

His idea was to find a way round or to force Santos to follow him. That way he, Brogan, would have the advantage and possibly surprise Santos. However, he had the feeling that Santos was not a man who was easily fooled or surprised. In fact, it very quickly became apparent that the way he had chosen was far from easy as it suddenly narrowed and rose steeply. However, being his usual pig-headed self, he refused to admit his error and he doggedly persisted with his chosen route. After some very tortuous twists and turns, he was beginning to wonder if he *was* doing the right thing. He did not have to wonder for very long.

'It is so nice to meet you once again, Señor McNally!' a familiar voice suddenly boomed out from somewhere above him. 'I think that you have made the wrong choice this time. Welcome to the only cemetery you will ever know.'

'Oh shit!' Brogan cursed loudly to himself. Santos plainly found this very funny as he laughed loudly.

As far as Brogan was concerned, this was plainly one of the few occasions in his life when he had made a big mistake. What made him more annoyed was the fact that his normally reliable senses had failed to detect the ambush. He sighed resignedly, slouched in his saddle and then looked up.

Santos was standing on a large rock about thirty feet above him. Two Indian men also stood on other rocks, one either side of narrow valley. He glanced back and saw a third Indian taking up position behind him. All four men had their rifles trained on him. He was well and truly trapped and it was not an experience he liked very much.

'I knew you would follow,' continued Santos, 'and I also knew that you would not attempt the other valley. I had deliberately left tracks heading that way but I knew that you would suspect an ambush. That is why I chose to wait here. I have learned something of the way your mind works. You are very predictable, Señor McNally, probably too predictable for your own good.'

'I guess that's one up to you, Santos,' said Brogan. 'So what you waitin' for? All it needs is one good shot.'

'True,' agreed Santos, 'and I shall take great pleasure in shooting you. However, I am still very curious as to why a man like you should do what you do. I have met drifters before but I have never met one who seems to care about others as you do. I think you would be better suited as a priest.'

'Me an' any god or gods have an understandin',' said Brogan. 'I don't help him or them an' they don't help me. It's worked pretty well so far.'

'But this time luck has deserted you,' said Santos with a laugh. 'I too have that same understanding. The difference between you and me is that I do not help anyone else either. In seeking to kill me you simply waste your time. I told you before that I am nobody, you are nobody and who cares what happens to a nobody. So, you get rid of me or someone like me sometimes and for a time the villagers of Santa Cruz live without any fear. The only trouble is it will not be long before someone else takes my place and the fear starts all over again. Like the cockroach, you could spend most of your life killing them but whenever you open a door, there is always another one. *Sí*, I know my worth, gringo, as I suspect you know yours. We both have our grand ideas which in reality are meaningless. Sometimes, as they say, it is better to live with the devil you know and not the one you do not know. Do I make sense to you, Señor McNally?'

'In a twisted sort of way,' agreed Brogan. 'But then that's the kind of thinkin' I'd expect from someone as twisted as you.'

'Call me twisted if you please, *señor*,' said Santos with a loud laugh. 'Words are cheap when made by a condemned man and they can cause me no harm. It is not me who is about to die.'

'Then I suggest you get on with it,' said Brogan. 'I hate to be kept waitin' around for anythin' an' I always said I'd like my own death to be quick when it came to my turn.'

'It had been my intention to kill you slowly but I have enjoyed the chase and I am a merciful man.' said Santos. 'It shall be as you wish, your death will be swift.' He raised his rifle. '*Adios*, Señor McNally . . .

Brogan moved swiftly and he managed to draw his Colt but the odds were very much against him and, although he was faster than most men, he could not move swiftly enough. He vaguely heard a shot followed by a searing pain to his head and nothing more.

What could only have been a few moments later, Brogan came to. He was on the ground alongside his horse and there was a painful throb in his head but at least he was still alive. His eyes opened briefly and in time to see Santos and two of the Indians descending the rocks as they made their way towards him. Where the third Indian was he did not know and at that moment did not care. He closed his eyes sufficiently to make it appear they were fully closed, and remained perfectly still. His Colt was close at hand.

He heard Santos talking to the Indians but still he waited. Suddenly he felt a boot dig into his ribs . . .

Brogan even surprised himself at the speed of his reaction and he obviously surprised the Indian whose boot kicked his ribs. He grabbed the offending foot and twisted with all the force he could muster. In almost the same instant, he managed to grab his Colt and, more by pure instinct than sight, he shot at a shadowy figure. His second shot was made with rather more clarity and a second Indian crashed to the ground. Suddenly, all went quiet.

He looked about and saw that the third Indian was running away towards the village. He made no attempt to stop him, there seemed little point.

The men he had shot were Pablo Santos and the other Indian. The first, whose foot he had seized, was lying on the ground with a gash to his head, the result of hitting his head on a rock, but was otherwise uninjured and alive. He was plainly expecting to be shot. Brogan kicked away the man's rifle and took a handgun from his waist which he also cast aside.

The second Indian was most definitely dead, shot through the head which was more due to luck than actual intention. Santos appeared to be alive although apparently badly injured by a shot to his chest. Brogan shook his head in an attempt to clear his throbbing pain and his sight, wiped his sleeve across his forehead to remove some blood, and stood over Santos.

'It looks like it was you who made the mistake this time,' said Brogan. 'Ain't nobody ever told you to make sure a man's dead before you approach him?'

'You might not have a pact with any god,' said Santos, smiling weakly and in obvious pain, 'but as I said before, gringo, the devil is with you. It has been a most enjoyable encounter, Señor McNally, and I have learned much, although I always believed that a gringo could teach me nothing. I shall not make the same mistakes again.'

'You just made the biggest mistake of your life,' said Brogan. 'I reckon you is all but dead. I don't think there's anythin' I can do for you. I don't think you'd even make it back to that village.'

'Sí, for once I agree with you and would not expect you to try and save me. I know I would not try to save your life,' rasped Santos. 'Now you can go back to the peons in Santa Cruz and tell them that I, Pablo Santos, the man the Mexican prisons could not keep and the Mexican army could not catch, has been defeated by a lone gringo. Sí, that is the hardest part of all to bear. That I should have been beaten by a gringo. You can also tell them that I shall be back. Perhaps not as Pablo Santos, this body is of no use any longer, but I shall return in some other form. However, the effect will be the same. Adios, Señor McNally ... for now!'

Santos sighed deeply, choked slightly, his eyes closed and his head lolled to one side. A slight trickle of blood oozed from his mouth and his nose. Brogan heeded his own advice and checked to make sure that he was indeed dead. In a strange way he even felt rather sad about it. He turned to the remaining Indian who was still on the ground and still terrified.

'*Vamanos!*' he commanded, not quite certain if that was the correct expression or not.

Correct or not, it certainly appeared to be enough for the Indian who suddenly leapt to his feet and followed his surviving companion back towards the village, leaving his guns behind. Brogan too mounted his horse and rode back down the narrow valley until he joined the wider one. He made no attempt to bury or hide the two bodies since he was quite certain that it would not be long before people from the village came to recover them. If they did not, at least he knew that the buzzards would get a good feed.

★ ★ ★

'So Pablo Santos is no more,' Padre Luis Salada said to Brogan when he was told of the death of the *bandido*. 'I am not sure if I should be glad or sad. I am happy for the people of this and other villages because they will not be troubled by Santos again, but I am sad that so many had to die in the process. Unfortunately that is the way things are. Life is rarely what we would like it to be.'

'You'd better believe it,' said Brogan. 'Having a religious faith is fine for most an' probably very necessary for a few, but I've never yet found it much use against a bullet. Bullets ain't got no religion an' they sure don't care who they kill. That's their job.'

Later that day the soldiers arrived in the village. Brogan recognized the sergeant and a good number of other men but the officer was a different and much younger man. Brogan's first instincts about the man were that he was also a very different character from the other officer. Plainly of aristocratic origins and apparently very full of his own self-importance, he made little secret of his contempt for the villagers and apparently had little regard for his men either.

'What happened to the other officer?' asked Brogan. 'I never did know his name. There never seemed much point in askin' him. He said that he might be arrested or somethin' for what happened.'

'At least he was right about something,' sneered the new officer. 'He is under arrest for gross dereliction of duty.' There was a definite note of sarcasm in his voice. 'How any man could be so careless in a god-forsaken place such as this I will never know. It is most likely that he will be shot for losing so many men. At the very least he will serve a long time in a military prison and then, should he survive, be turned out with nothing. His family will curse the day he was born. His shame will also be their shame.'

'Didn't the sergeant tell you what happened?' asked Brogan. 'He was there. They never stood a chance.'

'That was a situation of his own making,' sneered the officer. 'More importantly he disobeyed standing orders by not requesting permission to go beyond his area of command. The sergeant and the other men are not to blame, they were simply obeying the command of an officer, it is not their place to reason why.'

'This is what brings you to Santa Cruz now?' asked Padre Luis. 'You come just to tell us this?'

'I come just to let you know that I am now in command of this territory,' said the officer, bridling slightly at being questioned. 'I doubt you will see me very often . . . ' He looked about the village scornfully. 'I see nothing here to interest me or my men. You do not even have any attractive women. You have goats and some of my men might even prefer a goat to your women, but I am very particular about my women.' He looked at Brogan and sneered. 'I have been told of you, Señor McNally, and I do not like what I hear. You appear to believe that you are above the law and superior to officers of the Mexican army. That is not so, you are but a worthless drifter. I am told that you have killed Pablo Santos but I do not believe it. Where is your proof? We have only your word for such a thing. There is a reward for the capture dead or alive of Pablo Santos but do not think that you can collect this reward without proof and the only proof which is acceptable is the body of Pablo Santos. Even if it is true and Santos is dead, you will never collect the reward.'

'I ain't in the habit of tellin' lies,' said Brogan. 'I ain't interested in the reward either. That apart, I personally don't give a shit whether you believe me or not.'

'We shall see,' grunted the officer. 'I have heard stories that some money was hidden in Santa Cruz. I am also told that you have searched everywhere for it but have been unable to find it.'

'That is so, Excellency,' said the village headman, glancing at Padre

Luis. 'It can be nothing more than a story.'

'Just as I thought,' said the officer, seeming quite pleased that at least one man in the village recognized his position. 'There is no money and that is official, I have it on the authority of the governor. Now, tonight you will provide food for me and my men and anything else they need.'

'*Anything* else, Excellency?' asked the headman.

'*Sí, anything*,' replied the officer. 'Even an ugly woman or a goat can be attractive to a soldier who has been without for a long time. As for you, Señor McNally, in the name of the governor of this province, I am ordering you to leave Mexico. You have two days, no more. Should I learn that you are still here, I shall order your arrest and you will be sent to prison. Believe me, *señor*, Mexican prisons are not very nice places. I know, I worked in one for some time and it is not an experience even I would would wish to repeat.'

'I've done nothing wrong,' objected Brogan. 'What would be the charge?'

'Charge! Who needs a charge?' laughed the officer. 'Here in Mexico it is easy to find a reason to imprison someone. Sometimes it is not even necessary for a trial to take place. Please, for your own sake, Señor McNally, do not attempt to test me on this. I can assure you that you can only lose.'

Brogan did not doubt that the officer meant what he said and even he was not prepared to take on the military. To save any further problems for the villagers, he agreed to leave within the required two days.

Some time later the sergeant came to see the headman and the priest and assured them that the promise made by the previous officer would be honoured. The women of the village would not be molested. All he asked was that the new officer was not told of the arrangement. Should he hear of it, it was quite possible that he would order the molestation of the women. It seemed that this new officer was not at all popular with the soldiers.

The soldiers left early the following morning, the officer once again reminding Brogan that he had to leave the country. Brogan too decided that there was little point in remaining. Everything that could be done for the people of Santa Cruz had been done.

'It would seem that it is now official and the money does not exist,' said Padre Luis shortly before Brogan was due to leave. 'We could have paid you for what you have done for us.'

'Come to terms with your conscience then, have you?' said Brogan.

'You heard what the officer said, and he speaks in the name of the governor who also speaks in the name of El Presidente,' said the priest. 'There is no money, it is now official.'

'From the sound of that I'd say that you for one believe it's still here somewhere,' said Brogan.

'More than that, Señor McNally,'

said the priest with a broad grin. 'We were not idle while you were away. A woman gave birth to a stillborn baby and when such a thing happens we use a special grave since they have not been confirmed into the church. There are other such children in the grave. As we dug the hole again, we discovered a leather bag. It contained almost twenty-five thousand dollars, about half what we expected, but it is still a considerable amount of money. It was remembered that another child had been stillborn when the men were in the village. They obviously opened the grave while we were asleep.'

'And your conscience is quite clear?' queried Brogan.

'There can be no conflict of either the law or my conscience since, as you have heard for yourself, the money does not officially exist,' said the priest with a broad grin. 'I am sure that you also will not have any difficulty in accepting a donation from the village as a thank you for all your trouble. Will three thousand dollars cover your time and your trouble?'

'Just about right, I'd say,' said Brogan. 'Just a thought though. Won't people start askin' questions when you pay for things in American dollars?'

'Often, American dollars are preferred to pesos, but I see your point,' said the priest. 'I have a very good friend who owns a bank in Texas. I shall arrange with him to change most of the money into Mexican pesos.'

★   ★   ★

It was mid-morning the following day before Brogan was ready to leave Santa Cruz. How many of the villagers knew of the money Brogan did not know and did not ask. He suspected that information had been kept to those few who really needed to know, to keep the news as quiet as possible. With the best will in the world, there was always somebody who talked too much. Brogan also sensed that the money would be put to good use and not kept by the few who knew about it.

As he was about to leave, five Mexican men rode into the village and it was obvious that they were not simply riding through. Brogan had a sinking feeling in his stomach and his hand dropped to his Colt. The villagers ran to their houses to hide.

The apparent leader of the men sneered at Brogan and called to the priest and the headman. It seemed that he could speak no English.

'He says that he and his men are now in control of this and other villages,' said the priest. 'He demands that we provide food, drink and women. If we do not he will kill both me and the headman.'

'Oh shit, here we go again,' muttered Brogan. 'Pablo Santos said he would be back.'

'He also says that you are to hand over your guns,' continued the priest. 'If you do as he says you will not be harmed providing you leave the village straight away.'

'I seem to remember hearin' somethin' like that not long ago,' said Brogan. 'You can't expect me to agree can you?'

'There will be no need,' said the headman. 'We have not lost Pablo Santos just to have somebody else replace him, *señor*. I suggest that we walk slowly over to the tree.'

'What for?' asked Brogan.

'Do as I say and you will soon discover the reason,' said the headman.

Brogan shrugged and led his horse to the tree. Suddenly the air was filled with sound of gunfire and the five would-be *bandidos* fell to the ground.

Four young men emerged from the houses and slowly advanced on the men on the ground. They were plainly in no mood to be merciful as two of them shot two of the *bandidos* who were not dead.

'Well at least they've learned how to look after themselves,' said Brogan. 'My congratulations.'

'We have guns now,' said the

headman. 'We can now defend ourselves.

'Five more deaths,' sighed the priest,
although there was a faint smile playing
on his lips. 'So unnecessary, such a
waste.'

'You still have a conscience then?'
said Brogan.

'Conscience, Señor McNally?' replied
the priest, his smile breaking into a
broad grin. 'The Good Book says that it
is permissible to take an eye for an eye.
In that sense I use a liberal translation.
I have learned from you that faith and
good words are not enough on many
occasions. I have also learned that the
threat of violence is enough reason to
provoke a legitimate response. Anyway,
who is to know what happened? I have
never seen or heard of these men
before, in fact I do not think they really
existed. They are as but spirits in
transit, they needed help to step into
heaven, that is all. Did you not say that
Santos vowed to return in another
form? Santos is dead, you have killed

him yourself and since it is impossible to kill a dead man, what you have just witnessed cannot have happened.'

'Just like your money,' said Brogan with a broad grin. 'Maybe you'd better get them non-existent men into non-existent graves before anyone starts seeing ghosts.'

THE END

We do hope that you have enjoyed reading this large print book.

Did you know that all of our titles are available for purchase?

We publish a wide range of high quality large print books including:
Romances, Mysteries, Classics
General Fiction
Non Fiction and Westerns

Special interest titles available in large print are:
The Little Oxford Dictionary
Music Book, Song Book
Hymn Book, Service Book

Also available from us courtesy of Oxford University Press:
Young Readers' Dictionary
(large print edition)
Young Readers' Thesaurus
(large print edition)

For further information or a free brochure, please contact us at:
Ulverscroft Large Print Books Ltd.,
The Green, Bradgate Road, Anstey,
Leicester, LE7 7FU, England.
Tel: (00 44) **0116 236 4325**
Fax: (00 44) **0116 234 0205**

A TOWN CALLED TROUBLESOME

John Dyson

Matt Matthews had carved his ranch out of the wild Wyoming frontier. But he had his troubles. The big blow of '86 was catastrophic, with dead beeves littering the plains, and the oncoming winter presaged worse. On top of this, a gang of desperadoes had moved into the Snake River valley, killing, raping and rustling. All Matt can do is to take on the killers single-handed. But will he escape the hail of lead?